Jade is in Manhattan

Stylish, classy, fun and full of love.

Jade is in Manhattan

A Novella

Chartese Mitchell

Brighter Star Press

ISBN: 13: 978-0-692-12904-3 (Paperback)

ISBN: 10: 0-692-12904-9

Front cover image by Artist. Book design by Designer.

Printed in the United States of America. First printing, 2018.

Publisher

Brighter Star Press, LLC

ACKNOWLEDGEMENTS

I cannot express enough thanks to my support system for their continued assistance and encouragement: Kristine Nolan, my editor, and Mr. Sheer Genius, my cover designer. My completion of this book would not have been possible without you.

Finally, to my loving and supportive family, thank you for your support and encouragement throughout my writing and publishing process. You will forever have my deepest gratitude.

Prologue

Before moving to the Big Apple, Jade and her children, Jayden and Brittany, lived in a two-bedroom condo in Long Beach, California, which is right outside of LA. Her children attended school not too far from their home, which was very convenient, considering Jade worked only ten minutes away from their school, where she happened to manage one of Long Beach's upscale women's boutiques. Jade, a hard worker and dedicated mother, faced minor challenges with men. She juggled a demanding work schedule, aerobic activities, and her two active children.

With the responsibility of raising Jayden and Brittany on her own, Jade hadn't had much time for a love life. You would think as beautiful as she was that prince charming would have swept her off her feet by now!

The funny thing is that Jade hasn't had much success with finding her Mr. Right. Since the breakup with her high school sweetheart, Tyler, who happened to be her children's dad, Jade just continued to stay focused on work and the kids.

Before they went their separate ways, Tyler and Jade couldn't get enough of each other. They were one of the hottest couples in school. With Jade, being the cute cheerleader, and Tyler, the star player of their high school basketball team, the two became very popular. They had met at a school dance. Jade was wearing a beautiful black and white, off-the-shoulder dress, and Tyler was decked out in a black Christian Dior suit with a red tie to accent it. There was no doubt that they were the showstoppers at Wilson High.

After years of dating and after the birth of their two children, Jade and Tyler began to grow apart. Jade went on to major in fashion at a local fashion institute and became a stylist. Her interest in clothes and accessories became a big part of her and demanded a lot of dedication. Tyler went on to become a professional ball player, got married, and lives in Miami where his parents also reside.

Jade was also close to her family. She and the kids would always visit Mama and Papa during the holidays. However, when Jade was young, her parents didn't have a lot of money, but they always wanted the best for their little girl.

Jade's mother was a church-going woman and was very active in the community. She would sing at Sunday services and help serve dinner afterwards. Jade could always turn to her mama for advice about men and other life concerns. She would always reassure Jade by telling her what her mom used to say, "Love will come find you," and before she finished, Jade would join in to say it with her.

Papa was no rolling stone; in other words, he was honest, faithful, wise, and laid back, but somehow, he kept his sternness. He felt nobody was good enough for his Little J, which was the nickname he gave Jade when she was just a baby. Papa would look into her big, brown eyes and say, "That's my Little J."

Jade had a brother, Zack. After graduation, he moved to France to teach English as a second language. Jade and Zack didn't speak very often due to distance and busy schedules, but oh, how they loved one another! Growing up, they used to play all sorts of childhood games and couldn't wait until the holidays came around—especially Christmas. This was when all the family would gather together and have a good time.

"Those were the good ole days," they would say after reminiscing about their childhood past. Now, they're adults and have children of their own, and they say, "My, how time flies!"

Jade Moves to New York

1

Rushing through the busy streets of Manhattan, Jade and the kids are off to the airport to meet Tyler.

"Daddy! Daddy! Look! There's Daddy!" Brittany yelled out, pulling on Jade's arm.

"I see, sweetie! Thank God his flight was on time," Jade mumbled. "I guess your dad's meeting ended early," she said to the kids.

Tyler walked over to where they were standing. "Hello Jade," he said in that low, sexy voice she remembered as they talked on the phone until the wee hours of the night. He then leaned in and kissed her cheek.

Oh, no, he didn't, Jade thought to herself as she stood in awe. "Hello, Tyler," she then answered. "How was your flight?"

"Not too bad, considering I had to sit next to a talkative old lady," he answered with a chuckle.

"Oh, so, she must have sat in first class since that's how you travel, in style," said Jade.

Tyler grinned, "Yeah, she talked me to sleep though, with all her stories and how some guy named Charles proposed to her over a romantic dinner in Paris."

Jade laughed.

"Man, all this traveling has got a brother tired," Tyler said, running his fingers through his curly head. "Hey, how's my little mama been doing?" he asked while bending down to pick Brittany up.

"Fine, Daddy," she answered and began to tell him all about their new puppy, Skittles.

"You didn't," said Tyler, looking over at Jade.

"Yes, I did. I brought her home one evening as a surprise gift for the kids. We would always talk about getting a dog but could never decide on the breed. I didn't want anything too big, so I found us a cute little dog that doesn't grow much," she said, looking over at Jayden.

"Huh. I see. Maybe I'll get to meet Skittles one day," said Tyler.

He walked closer to where Jayden was standing. "So, Jayden, my boy, how are those jumpers coming along? I heard you are the school's most valuable player this year."

"Oh, I still got it, Dad! You have to come see me play again. The coach has been really impressed with my dunking skills too," Jayden said excitedly.

"That's my boy," Tyler said, pulling Jayden under his arm. "That's what I like to hear, son."

Tyler then turned in Jade's direction. "Well, Jade, it seems like you and the kids have been doing really well. Oh, and by the way, you're still looking good," he said jokingly and smiled.

"I know, but thank you," she responded, smiling as Tyler joked. "So, how's your family?" she asked, quickly changing the subject.

"Good! Everything's going well back home, and it's been an alright season for the team too."

"Glad to hear all is well," said Jade while she adjusted the straps on Brittany's pink Tweety backpack. "There you go, baby!"

Jade looked back up at Tyler. "That girl has gotten taller over the last few months," Jade said, shaking her head.

"Yes, she has grown since the last time I saw them," he said, picking up his luggage. "So, who's the new man in your life?"

Jade put her hand on her hip. "Excuse me?" Jade questioned. *What does he want to know for?* She thought to herself then smiled at his curiosity.

"Sorry, or should I ask, what is new in Jade's life?" he asked, changing the question around.

Before she could answer, their flight was called. "Okay, kids, it's time to board!"

"Bye, Mommy!" said Brittany.

"Bye, baby!" After looking at the flight schedule, Jade turned to Jayden. "Will you do me a favor? Look after your little sister," Jade asked while fixing the collar on his white, short-sleeve polo shirt.

"Yes, Mom," he answered. Then he looked over at Brittany with a silly grin on his face.

Jade kissed the kids on the cheek then turned to Tyler. "Take care."
"You too," said Tyler.

She waved goodbye and blew kisses as they boarded the plane. "Have a great summer, you guys, and be sure to call me!"

"Okay!" they both yelled then walked toward the boarding ramp with Tyler leading the way.

"I love you!" Jade yelled as she continued watching them through the huge windows. After their plane took off, she began walking back to her SUV. A tear rolled down Jade's face as she took out her cell phone to call her best friend, Sasha, who she met while attending fashion school some years ago. Now they work together.

Ring! Ring!

"Hey, girly," said Sasha.

"How did you know it was me?"

"Caller ID, remember?" Sasha answered and began laughing.

Wiping the tear from her face, Jade exclaimed, "Whatever! So, are you working today?"

"On this nice, hot, sunny Saturday? Nope. I told Zoe I wasn't coming in today and that I have some business to take care of," answered Sasha.

"Oh, really? What kind of business do you have to take care of that can't wait until you get off work?" asked Jade.

"Let's see…shopping, getting my hair, nails, and feet done. Did I mention a full-body massage too?"

"Girl, you not right!" Jade said, laughing on the other end of the phone.

"Girly, I have to look good because Mike and I are going to Ocean Seas tonight. Oh, yeah, he's bringing a friend from work, and he's single too," Sasha added.

Shaking her head, Jade said, "Don't even think about it!"

"Come on! It'll be fun!"

"Well, I don't have the kids since they're staying the summer with Tyler, and it has been a while since I've been to Ocean Seas. Okay, what time should I meet you guys there?"

"Eight o'clock," Sasha answered with a big smile on her face.

"See you then, but for now, I'm going to work. I know Zoe needs my help, and besides, we have new dresses arriving today," said Jade.

"You're trying to make me feel bad, right?"

"Yes," she answered and started laughing.

"Bye, girly," said Sasha, hanging up the phone.

Jade arrived at the boutique. "Hey, Zoe!" she said happily.

"Hey. Am I glad to see you! Sasha called out this morning, and we're expecting those dresses to arrive anytime today. Lola just called to see if they came in yet. You know, they are having that big charity event she's hosting, and she wanted something cute to wear," said Zoe anxiously.

"Speaking of outings, I'm going to Ocean Seas with Sasha and Mike tonight," Jade said excitedly.

Zoe looked rather surprised. "What? Isn't there a saying that three is a crowd?" she asked before chuckling. "Just kidding. Maybe you'll find yourself a man there."

"Oh, well, did I mention that Mike's bringing a friend along from work?" Jade grinned as she folded a pair of designer jeans.

"Really?" Zoe questioned. "Is he cute?"

"I don't know... I haven't met him yet," answered Jade. "But we'll see tonight." They both giggled.

"So, what are you doing after work, Zoe?"

"Remember that guy I met when I went jogging in Central Park last Sunday? Well, we're going to watch movies at his house tonight," Zoe answered with a grin.

"That sounds like fun! Make sure you take some popcorn," teased Jade. "Ha! Ha! Ha!" Zoe laughed.

"Well, let's get these dresses hung up, so we can call it a wrap."

"I agree," said Zoe.

The day went by as Jade and Zoe prepared for closing. "Goodnight, girl. Have fun," said Jade.

"You too!" said Zoe, "And don't forget to tell me all about it on Monday!"

"I won't," said Jade as she walked down the street to peek in the window of Manhattan's Fine Art Gallery. Jade always had a good eye for fine art and famous paintings. She would gaze in the window from time to time at an art piece displayed on the wall, which happened to be very expensive and too much for Jade's pocketbook. *Such a unique piece of art,* Jade thought, while trying to see the price tag from outside. *I wonder how much they want for it.*

"Oh, my! Look at the time!" Jade softly yelled after looking at her phone. "I have to go home to get myself ready for tonight." Jade drove off in her silver Benz SUV and headed home to change her clothes.

It was about quarter to seven when Sasha walked in from a full day of pampering. She tossed her shopping bags on the couch and flopped down in the chair next to it. "Huh…" she sighed. "What a day!" She then heard her phone ringing.

I wonder who that is. Sasha questioned and reached for the phone. "Hello?"

"Hey, baby!" It was Mike.

"Hi, sweetie," said Sasha.

"I'll be there to pick you up at 7:30," he said.

"Okay, sounds good. Oh, and Mike, I can't wait to see you tonight." "Neither can I, baby." They hung up the phone.

Sasha grabbed her bags and ran in her bedroom. She dumped everything on the bed, trying to decide what to wear. *I think this would be a good choice. Mike won't be able to keep his eyes off me in this dress.* She picked out a sexy, red, bodycon dress and red, strappy, 4-inch heels to match. She went in the bathroom to run her shower. "I'm so excited! This is going to be a fun night!"

Jade walked in the door of her luxury, three-bedroom apartment. "Hey, Skittles! What you been up to?" she asked while cuddling Skittles in her arms. "Awww... Your bowl is empty! You must be hungry. Let mama get you something to eat," she said and poured food into the bowl.

Jade then turned on her music and opened a bottle of water. *A shower sure sounds good right about now.* She headed to her bedroom, sat at the edge of her bed, and took off her shoes to massage her feet. "Ummm... that feels good. I guess I'll hop in the shower really quick before Sasha calls, bugging me about being ready. I know how she is when it's time to go somewhere," she mumbled.

Jade then began undressing to get in the shower. The phone rang, but she couldn't hear it over the music and with the shower running. The answering machine picked up: "This is Jade, Brittany, and Jayden. We're not home. Please leave a message after the tone. Thank you! *Beep.*"

It was 7:30 when Jade walked out of the shower. The blinking red light indicated that she had missed a call. Jade played the message while she got dressed. It was Sasha. "Girly, where are you? It's 7:30, and Mike will be here to get me soon. I wanted to tell you where we are going to be sitting. So, call me, okay? Bye!"

Jade called Sasha back. "Hey, girl, I was in the shower when you called."

"Oh, okay... Well, here's the plan," said Sasha. "We're going to be sitting over in the private dining section. So, when you are on your way in, call me, and I'll guide you to us," she added.

"Alright," Jade replied.

"By the way, what are you wearing?" asked Sasha.

"A black cocktail dress and black pumps," answered Jade.

"Cute! I know Mike's friend won't be disappointed."

"Bye, Sasha!" Jade yelled.

"Okay, see you soon," said Sasha. After hanging up the phone, Sasha heard a knock on the door. "Oh, that must be Mike… Coming!" Sasha yelled, checking herself out in her full-length mirror. She slowly opened the door.

"Wow… baby, you look stunning," said Mike. He then kissed Sasha on the lips.

"Thanks, honey," she said, twirling around so he could dress she was wearing. "Well, we better get going now," Sasha said and grabbed her purse.

"Or, we can stay here," said Mike playfully and pulled Sasha close.

"No, we can't," she said gently sliding from his strong arms.

"You're right. Tony will be meeting us there soon. I asked him to wait in the front lobby until we arrive," Mike replied. Sasha and Mike then drove off in his sports car and headed to the restaurant.

Jade walked out of her building. "Hi, Mr. Franklin," she said to the bellman standing outside the door.

"Hello there, Ms. Taylor," he responded. "My, my…. don't you look lovely tonight?"

"Why, thank you," said Jade as she stood next to him while waiting on her vehicle to come around.

"Here it comes now, Ms. Taylor," said Mr. Franklin.

"Hey, Sean," Jade said to the attendant who pulled her SUV from the parking garage.

"Hello... Ms. Taylor," said Sean in a flirtatious manner.

"Behave yourself, Sean. You know I'm old enough to be your mother," said Jade before smiling.

Mr. Franklin laughed. "You heard the lady," he said.

Jade got in, and Sean closed the door for her. "You have fun tonight," said Mr. Franklin, "and be safe, you hear?"

"I will," replied Jade. "You all have a good night yourselves," she said and pulled off with her hand waving out the window.

"That's one beautiful lady," mumbled Mr. Franklin.

Mike and Sasha arrived at Ocean Seas. "What's happening, Tony?" asked Mike as he reached to shake his hand.

"Not too much, man," Tony answered. "This must be the lovely lady you speak of all the time."

"Yes, this is Sasha."

"Nice to meet you, Ms. Sasha," said Tony. "Mike has told me a lot about you. Must be nice working in one of New York's most expensive boutiques."

"Yes, it is. The quality of our clothing is very rare to find unless you're willing to go to Paris or Italy to purchase them. Now remember, you're paying for the style and quality of our clothes," answered Sasha, smiling back.

"She knows her stuff," said Tony as they slowly approached the hostess desk.

"Mike, Sasha, glad to see you again," said Layla, their hostess.

"Hey, Layla, how have you been?" asked Sasha.

"Well, let me put it to you like this: I still have a job, and the kids are fine. So, I'm doing alright," she answered.

"That's right, girly!" said Sasha in agreement.

"Well, it's good seeing you again too. Let me show you to your table.

Right this way!" said Layla.

Jade pulled up in front of Ocean Seas Restaurant and stepped out of her Benz. "Good evening, ma'am," said the parking attendant, standing at the entrance.

"Good evening," Jade answered and handed him the keys, thanking him. She then took out her cell phone to call Sasha. "Hey girl... I'm here!"

"Good. We've been waiting on you," said Sasha. "We're sitting in the private dining section where we had your 30th birthday party."

"Okay, see you in a bit," said Jade. She hung up the phone and walked through the doors. "Hey, Layla! How have you been?"

"I've been well. Busy with work and the kids—that's all. You know how that is," answered Layla.

Jade smiled. "Girl, you don't have to tell me twice."

"Well, let me show you to your table. I know your party's waiting."

Jade followed behind her to their table. "Hello, everyone," Jade said.

"Hey, glad you can join us," replied Mike.

"Hey, girly..." said Sasha as she stood and gave Jade a hug.

"Good evening," said Tony as he also stood and reached to kiss Jade's hand. "This is my co-worker, Tony Jacobs," said Mike.

"Very beautiful," Tony replied intrigued with her looks. "Let me help with that," he said, pulling out Jade's chair.

"Thank you," she replied as she took her seat. Immediately, Jade noticed the diamond ring on the middle finger of Tony's right hand. It looked as if it cost anywhere between five and seven grand! *That's a really expensive looking ring he's wearing,* she thought.

Then a waiter walked up to their table. "Can I get anyone a drink?"

"I'll have a glass of chardonnay, please," answered Sasha.

"I'll have one also," said Jade.

"I'll take a glass of merlot," said Mike.

"For you, sir?" asked the waiter as he looked over at Tony.

"May I have a glass of your finest cabernet sauvignon, please?" Tony replied. "Yes, sir. I'll be right back with your drinks," replied the waiter.

They all looked over at Tony. "Hmm... you must know your wines," said Jade.

"Yes, a little," Tony replied. "I travel a lot on business, and during my visits, I make it my duty to eat at fine restaurants."

"I see..." said Jade. "You have good taste in clothes also. Is that an Italian designer shirt?"

"Yes, it is," answered Tony, "and you, my dear, know clothes."

Jade smiled. "Yes, I'm the manager of Chic Couture, a clothing boutique on 59th Street."

"That's right! Mike did mention you and Sasha worked in an upscale ladies' clothing store."

"Boutique!" Jade and Sasha yelled at the same time. Tony chuckled.

The waiter came back to the table with their drinks. "Are you all ready to order yet?" he asked.

"Baby, what would you like?" Mike asked Sasha.

"Uhm ... let me see. I think I'll have the grilled pink salmon, please," she said.

"That sounds good. I'll have the same," said Mike.

"For you, ma'am?" asked the waiter as he looked over at Jade.

"Oh... I will have your shrimp linguine alfredo," she answered.

"Sir?" asked the waiter, now looking over in Tony's direction.

"Ah, yes... I'll have the filet mignon—medium rare, please."

"Coming right up," said the waiter.

"Thank you," said Jade.

"My pleasure, ma'am," he replied.

"So, Tony, that's a very expensive looking ring you have there," said Jade.

"This old thing?" he said, looking at his hand. Sasha and Mike checked it out also.

"I thought you and Mike were in the same line of work," Jade said.

"Well ... I do have a little side business of my own. You know how that is."

Jade looked at Sasha and nodded. "Yeah…I guess there's nothing wrong with a little side business," Jade replied. Mike looked kind of surprised but didn't say anything.

"So, Jade, I hear you and Sasha go way back. How long have the two of you known each other?" Tony asked.

"Oh, since fashion school," said Jade.

"Yeah, my girl and I have been through a lot together. She's like a sister to me," Sasha added.

"That's nice," said Tony, taking a sip of his wine. The waiter came back with their food.

"Umm... that looks good," said Mike as the waiter set the plates in front of them.

"Thank you," said Sasha.

"You're quite welcome, ma'am," the waiter replied. "Enjoy your meal."

Jade took a look around the table, then she bowed her head to say a prayer over the food. "Amen." Sasha and Mike repeated. Then they all looked over at Tony.

"Yes... Amen," he, too, repeated.

"My... this sure smells good," said Mike.

"It sure does," said Tony as he fumbled with his napkin.

"Is everything okay?" asked Jade.

Sasha looked over at Tony. "Yes, I'm good," he replied. "It's been a little while since I've prayed before I ate."

"Oh... maybe you should do it more often," said Jade. "It's a really good habit."

Tony smiled at Jade's remark. "You're right. I should," he replied.

"Well, let's eat," said Mike.

"I agree," said Sasha.

"Um... this is good," said Tony. "How long have you guys been coming here?"

"Every chance we get. This actually used to be our meeting place every Friday night," answered Sasha. "My girls and I would get all styled up to come here and have a delicious entree."

"Man, the food is great here, and the atmosphere is so chill," Mike added.

"Oh, yeah… Jade, did you know Mike, who is the Executive Director of their firm—and Tony, the Chief of Finance, just landed one of the biggest marketing contract deals?" asked Sasha.

"No, I didn't. This is my first time hearing the good news," answered Jade. "Wow! We ought to be celebrating!"

"Yeah, it was a piece of cake after they saw the new products we were offering," said Mike.

"So, Tony, how do you like working with such a great guy?" Jade asked.

"Oh, if you're talking about Mike, he's the best. He has covered my butt many of times, and we've learned a lot from each other over the years."

"Hey, guys, I would like to propose a toast to the two number-one business deal makers around," said Sasha as she raised her glass.

"Hear, hear!" They all raised their wine glasses in the air.

"So, Tony, tell us a little more about that side business of yours," Sasha inquired.

"Well, there's not much to tell," he answered.

"Sure, there is," said Sasha. "Do you work at a bank or something part-time? Sell cars on the side? I know! You sell jewelry, right?" Sasha questioned.

"Uhm, from the size of that diamond, that would have been my guess," said Jade.

Mike had a surprised look on his face again. "Ladies! Give the guy a break."

"No, it's okay," said Tony. "I actually am a dealer, but not a car or jewelry dealer."

They all looked confused. "Okay, would you like to share with us what you do?" asked Jade.

"I'm in the home furnishing business," said Tony with a grin.

"Oh, that's nice," said Sasha as she ate the remainder of her dinner. "So, you can hook me up with a good deal, then, right?"

Tony grinned again. "I'm pretty sure we can work out something," he answered.

"Man, I didn't know you sell home furniture," said Mike. Tony remained quiet and took a sip of his wine. Jade happened to notice his silence.

"Wow, a businessman with good taste. That's alright with me," said Jade, "I love a man that's business-minded." Tony smiled then took another sip of his wine. "So, Tony, maybe you can show me some nice decorative pieces one day. I could use some advice on a portrait I've been looking at," said Jade.

"I would like that," said Tony.

Later that evening…."Well, it's getting late, and I should be going," said Jade, and she stood to shake Tony's hand.

"It was nice meeting you, lovely lady," he said.

Mike checked the time on the designer watch that Sasha gave him for his last birthday. "Yeah, baby, we should be going too."

Sasha stood as Mike placed her shawl over her shoulders. "Thanks, sweetie," she said.

"This was nice. Thanks for inviting me out," said Jade.

"You know, I got you, girly," said Sasha.

"I know, girl," said Jade, then she hugged Sasha and Mike goodbye. "Goodnight, Layla." They all said before leaving out the door.

"You come back, and see me, you hear?" she replied.

"You bet!" answered Mike.

"So, Jade, is it possible for us to see each other again?" asked Tony, quickly walking to catch up with her. Before Jade could answer, he handed her his business card. "Here, you think about it, and give me a call if you like. I'll be waiting," said Tony with a smile, and he closed her car door behind her. Jade shook her head side to side and drove off.

<h1 style="text-align:center">2</h1>

"Good morning, everyone!" Jade spoke when she walked into the boutique. "Good morning," said Zoe and Sasha, both smiling from ear to ear.

"What are those big smiles for?" asked Jade with a look of curiosity on her face.

"So, how was dinner last night?" asked Zoe as she teased Jade about her night out.

"It was nice," she answered. "I'm glad I was able to get out and do something different from my usual routine—but you still didn't answer my question," Jade added. "Why the smiles?"

"Well, we think someone has a little crush on you," said Sasha.

"Really?" replied Jade as she walked over to the register, noticing a bouquet of flowers. "Such beautiful yellow flowers. Who are they for?"

"You!" Sasha and Zoe both yelled.

"Me? Who in the world sent me flowers?" asked Jade.

"Let's see. There's a card attached," said Zoe. "My sweet lady, I just wanted to put a smile on that beautiful face of yours today. Signed, Tony. Aw... That's so sweet."

Jade remained speechless.

"Wow, girly! What did you all talk about after we left last night?" asked Sasha. "It's obvious he wants to get to know you better," said Zoe.

"Yeah, that's just it. He asked me last night if we can see each other again."

"What did you say?" asked Sasha.

"I didn't say anything."

"What do you mean you didn't say anything?" asked Zoe.

"That man was *fine* and smelled good too," said Sasha.

"I know, but he caught me by surprise," replied Jade. "Plus, he's a little too flashy for me, and did you see the ring he had on? I know it cost a little over five grand," said Jade.

"So, he has money. That's a good thing," said Zoe.

"Yes, it is, but I just don't know about this," replied Jade.

"Oh, give the man a chance. He did send you some beautiful flowers," said Zoe, going over to smell the bouquet.

"He sure did," said Jade giggling. "Okay, okay. Maybe one date won't hurt."

"Well, aren't you going to thank him for the flowers?" asked Sasha as she softly pushed Jade near the phone.

Zoe then rushed over to listen while Jade placed the call.

"Hello. This is Tony speaking."

"Hi, Tony. This is Jade. We met last night at Ocean Seas."

"I know who you are - that pretty lady that sat across from me at the table." Jade blushed. Sasha and Zoe smiled at his compliment.

"I wanted to thank you for the flowers you sent me this morning." "Flowers? What flowers?"

Jade looked confused. "The flowers that I received with a note attached saying, 'Signed Tony.' "

"Oh... those flowers," he said with a soft chuckle. "You're welcome, sweet lady. Pretty flowers for a pretty lady."

"So, it was you!" said Jade as she began to smile. "They're really beautiful." "I'm sorry for teasing you, but I did make you smile again, didn't I?"

Jade blushed.

"So, does this mean you'll have dinner with me again? Just the two of us?"

Sasha and Zoe nodded their heads in the background.

"Sure. How can I turn down dinner with such a nice guy?" replied Jade. "Great. What about Thursday evening?"

"Sounds good," she said. Sasha and Zoe giggled.

"I'll pick you up from the boutique at 7 o'clock," said Tony.

"Okay, I'll see you then." She hung up the phone and looked over at her smiling friends.

"Jade has a date!" sang Sasha and Zoe, teasing her while dancing around the boutique.

"Okay, back to work!" said Jade. "Y'all are not right." Then they all giggled—even Jade.

"Oh, Miss Zoe, you are not off the hook," said Sasha.

"Yeah! How was your movie with what's-his-name?" asked Jade.

"His name is Keith, and we had a wonderful time together," answered Zoe. "Okay, girly. So, get to the good stuff. Did he kiss you?" asked Sasha. "Well, did he?" asked Jade as she looked over at Zoe.

"Y'all are so nosey!" said Zoe, then she walked to the back of the boutique to get a box.

"You know he did," Sasha and Jade whispered.

"I heard that!" yelled Zoe from the back room. "And can I get some help, please?" she asked, struggling to carry a box to the display table.

Jade ran over to help. "Here, let's sit this on the round table in the center," she said.

Sasha walked over to help take the dresses out of the box to prepare for steaming. "Mama Mia," she said while holding a cute floral dress in front of her. "Oooh... girlies. I like this."

"That is cute," said Zoe.

"I believe that's the dress that was worn by that well-known model in the show last month," said Jade.

"I think you're right," Zoe said. "Oh, by the way, yes, he did kiss me." "Well, can he kiss?" asked Jade.

"It was alright," Zoe answered. Sasha and Jade looked at each other then at Zoe.

"Okay... he kissed me like a prince would his princess," she said with a big smile.

"Uhmm hmm!" yelled Sasha. "You know, Mike's a good kisser too," Sasha added.

Jade remained quiet as she began unpacking the box that Zoe brought out. Then she looked up at Sasha and Zoe. "It's been a while since I've been kissed by a man," said Jade.

"That's okay, girly," replied Sasha. "Tony might be the man to pop a big one on you." Jade smiled.

"Well, we better get these dresses steamed and hung up. Lola will be here soon to pick one out for her big charity event this weekend," said Zoe.

"You're right. Let's get busy," said Jade.

Zoe glanced out the window. "Look! Here comes Mrs. Jenkins, the one who's married to that wealthy realtor that only sells the biggest luxury homes you'd ever dream of living in."

"What? Did she just step out of that candy apple red convertible?" asked Sasha.

"Check out those fancy stiletto pumps she's wearing—and matching purse too!" said Jade.

"That Mr. Jenkins really spoils her," said Sasha.

"Shh... here she comes," said Zoe.

"Hello, Mrs. Jenkins." They all spoke when she walked in the door.

"Good day, ladies," she said as she began browsing through the dresses that were on the rack.

"Can we help you find something, Mrs. Jenkins?" asked Jade.

"Oh, no, dear. I'm just fine, but thank you."

"How's Mr. Jenkins doing these days?" asked Sasha.

"He's still busy as usual," Mrs. Jenkins answered. "You know how it is working with those high-nose clients. You're on their schedule," she said while still browsing.

"Yes, we do." They all answered.

"My, those are some gorgeous dresses you have there," Mrs. Jenkins said, looking over at another rack. "May I try these?" she asked as she held one up to her body.

"Sure, help yourself. They just arrived this morning," said Jade.

"Can I start a fitting room for you, Mrs. Jenkins?" asked Zoe.

"Please do," Mrs. Jenkins answered as she handed the dresses she picked out over to Zoe.

"Nice choices," Zoe said, then she hung them on the outside of the fitting room door.

Mrs. Jenkins then grabbed a tan chiffon neck scarf from the shelf. "This is the color I've been looking for. It will go really lovely with that tan dress I bought from here last week," she said.

"I think you're right, Mrs. Jenkins. I believe Jade was the one who helped you pick that cute dress out," said Zoe.

"Yes, she did, but I don't remember seeing this scarf the last time I was here. Are they new arrivals?" asked Mrs. Jenkins.

"Yes, they came in from Paris with some other designer accessories," answered Jade as she overheard the conversation.

"Yeah, like these stylish shades I have on," said Sasha as she pranced in front of the mirror in a pair of black, gold-trimmed sunglasses.

"Those are hot," said Zoe.

"I know, girly. Aren't they?" Sasha replied.

"Okay, ladies, I'm ready to try on my items now," said Mrs. Jenkins as she headed over to the fitting room.

"Let me get that for you," said Zoe while pulling open the fitting room door for her.

"Thank you, dear," she said.

"You're welcome. Let us know if you need anything else," Zoe added. Jade pulled out her cell phone to make a call.

"Who are you calling?" asked Sasha.

"Niecy over at Classy Lady Salon and Day Spa. I want to look good for my date on Thursday night," said Jade.

"I agree, girly! Go get yourself all beautiful for that man," said Sasha.

"Hello. Classy Lady Salon. Niecy speaking. How may I help you?" "Hi, Niecy, this is Jade. I need to make an appointment for Thursday

afternoon."

"Sure, Jade. Thursday's fine. Are we doing it during your lunch break again?" asked Niecy.

"You know it," replied Jade. They both giggled.

"Okay, I've got you down for twelve o'clock."

"Thanks. You're a lifesaver," said Jade.

"No problem. See you Thursday."

"Okay. Bye." Jade hung up the phone. "Good, that's out the way. Now, what am I going to wear?" she asked Sasha and Zoe.

"Girly, you know, we're going to make sure you look stunning before you leave out of here Thursday night," said Sasha.

"We'll pick out something really sassy, but later because we have customers coming in," said Zoe.

Sasha and Jade looked over at the door as two ladies dressed in business suits walked in. "Welcome to Chic Couture! My name is Jade. Please let me know if we can help you find something," she said.

"So, you're Jade," said one of the ladies as she extended her arm to shake Jade's hand.

"Yes, I am," Jade replied. "Can I help you?"

"We have heard so much about your boutique and wanted to talk with you about doing an article in our next month's issue of *Styles Inc.* magazine. We are speaking with some of New York's top-ranked ladies' boutique owners and managers, and Chic Couture was in the ranking."

"I'm sorry, but we didn't get your names," said Sasha.

"Of course. My name is Kori. This is Kim, and here are our business cards. We would love to see your boutique featured in our upcoming issue, and we'd love it if you could come to our office for an interview if you're interested," said Kori.

"Well, it was nice meeting you ladies today. I will have my assistant, Sasha, give you a call next week to set a date," replied Jade.

"Sounds good," said Kori.

"You mind if we look around?" Kim asked.

"Not at all. Help yourself," Jade answered.

Mrs. Jenkins walked out the fitting room and over to the register with a red dress in her hand. "Will this be all for you, Mrs. Jenkins?" asked Zoe before ringing up her dress.

"Yes," she answered, "and thanks for all your help, dear."

"My pleasure. It's always nice seeing your friendly face," said Zoe.

"Look. Here comes Lola now," said Sasha.

"Good day, everyone," Lola said as she strolled in the door.

"Hi, Lola. We were expecting you," said Jade. "The dresses are over here." Jade walked her to the dress section of the boutique. "We have a beautiful selection of sleek Couture gowns in also," Jade mentioned.

"This is nice," said Lola as she held a black satin, lace-trimmed dress up in front of her.

"That is nice. Would you like to try it on?" asked Jade.

"Yes, please," answered Lola as she followed Jade to the fitting room. "I'll let you see how it fits after I get it on," she added.

"Here, you may like this also. It's a little shorter," said Jade as she handed her a pretty white dress with gray and black flowers.

"Oh, I like this too. I'll try it on next. Thanks."

"You're welcome." Jade walked over to the register and smelled her flowers. "You know, the last time I was sent flowers this pretty was on Mother's Day a few years ago from this tall, handsome man named Blaine Thomas," said Jade as she reminisced about their time together.

"I believe you told me about him one night when I was out of town visiting my sister in Puerto Rico," said Sasha.

"Okay, well, tell me," said Zoe after overhearing the conversation. "It sounds like you two were in love."

"You could say that," Jade replied. "It all started like this: One day, I was admiring this beautiful painting at Manhattan's Fine Art Gallery over on Fifth Avenue. Then Blaine walked up beside me and said, 'This is one exquisite piece of work here.' I agreed with his comment without even looking up to see who said it. Then he said, 'It's almost as gorgeous as you are.' I looked up and saw this tall, fine man standing right beside me. I was in awe as I looked around to see if he was really talking to me. I smiled, of course, said thank you, and continued admiring the painting. He asked if I came here often because he saw me taking notes on my notepad and would have remembered seeing someone as attractive as me. I said, yes, what about you?"

"What did he say after you said that?" asked Zoe.

"Yeah, girly, tell us. What did he say next?" said Sasha.

"In the sexiest voice a man could have, he said, 'A woman is like a rose: delicately picked as she is carefully chosen.' "

"Aww... that is so beautiful," said Zoe.

"Wow… girly, he sounds like a true gentleman," said Sasha.

"Yes, he was," said Jade as she began to smile.

"Go on," said Lola as she stepped out of the fitting room with the dress Jade gave her to try on.

"Oh, that really looks nice on you, Lola," said Jade.

"Thanks. I like this one too," Lola replied. "I'll take them both. Okay, now, finish your story. This is interesting; plus, I like love stories." They all laughed.

"Okay," said Jade. "Then he introduced himself as Blaine Thomas. Oh, how I loved his name. It's masculine and fits him so well."

"Did you two ever date?" asked Zoe.

"Yes, and he was so good to me. I mean, this man would go above-and- beyond to please me. On our first date, he picked me up in a black limo. It was laid out—I tell you! When I got in, there was a red rose laying on the seat. So, I picked it up, said thank you, and sat down. Then, I was offered something to drink as we headed to our destination. The conversation we had was so intriguing that I even found out he's a lover of art just as I am."

"Really?" questioned Sasha.

"Yes, really," said Jade. "Let me finish. So, we pulled up to Riverbank Park, where a helicopter was sitting, and a man was standing."

"No, he didn't," said Lola.

"Yes, he did," said Jade. "Ladies, I looked at that fine man and shook my head, 'No way!' He smiled, took my hand, and told me, 'Come on. It'll be okay,' and that he'd made reservations for two at a very nice restaurant he wanted to take me to. I was so nervous and thrilled all at the same time. 'Lord, get me through this,' I prayed to myself. He was such a gentleman throughout the whole night, making me feel secure."

"Wow... I wonder if my friend would do something like that for me," said Zoe.

"Has he yet?" asked Lola.

"No, nothing like that."

"Then he ain't gonna!" they all said together and laughed.

"Oh, hush. He may one day," Zoe replied.

"Well, Mike did something like that for me too. He took me on a hot air balloon ride for our one-year anniversary," said Sasha.

"That was so nice of him. Now, let her finish," said Lola, waving her hand for Jade to continue. "Sorry, but I really want to hear the rest before I leave."

Sasha pouted her bottom lip out and turned her head the other way. They all began to laugh.

"After that night, we started spending a lot of time together. I even cooked for him, and y'all know if I invite you over for dinner, then I must really like you."

"What? You cook?" asked Zoe.

"Yes, I have kids to feed, don't I?" replied Jade. "I know! I was just kidding," said Zoe.

Jade smiled and continued. "That night, Blaine gave me a massage that was out-of-this-world! Then, I, of course, with my healing hands, returned the favor, and he was well pleased. We really had some fun times together. He was my friend, and eventually, we fell in love. Blaine was wonderful, and did I mention he loved the kids? I never knew I could love like that again before I met him. He was such a good man. I can go on-and-on. Oh, the things he did for me. Like one night, when we were out of town on a mini vacation in Jamaica, he planned this romantic dessert for us at the beach. He had candles to light our path that led to a white table with red rose petals sprinkled on it. There were two lit candles, two wine glasses, a bottle of champagne, a plate of strawberries, and a bowl of warm chocolate. I was so surprised at all he had done. Then I began hearing soft music playing, so I turned around and saw a group of men serenading as they approached us. He must have signaled for them to come out when I wasn't looking."

"Wow, that sounds so romantic," said Sasha.

"Yes, it was, and the walk along the beach was also," said Jade, "but that was Blaine: a romancer. He knew just what to do… I remember when my old car broke down and needed fixing. He insisted on paying for the repairs. Blaine refused to see me without transportation for too long. He even asked if I wanted another car, but, of course, I refused it. That was just the way Blaine was. He always made me feel like a lady, and second to God, I was the most important person in his life. Now Blaine wasn't the jealous type, but he was very protective of me. Blaine was like an angel. He always made sure I was okay. We used to have so much fun together. Oh, how I miss that man."

"So, where is he now?" asked Lola.

"Well, he had to go out of town for a while for his job. It actually called him away for a long period of time."

"So, is that why y'all are not together today?" asked Zoe.

"Yes, it was unexpected, which means our physical contact would be too limited. I loved him, but we both agreed I should go on with my life, so I did."

"I understand that, girly," said Sasha before walking over to console her. "That was the end of that, and we haven't spoken since," explained Jade.

"Hey, let's see if we can find you something to wear on your date with Mr. Bling," said Sasha, playfully teasing Jade. They all laughed.

"See, that's not right," replied Jade.

"I was just joking with you. He seems like a nice guy," said Sasha.

"Hey, what about this?" asked Zoe as she held up a pair of skinny jeans, a white designer t-shirt, and a black blazer.

"That's cute. You can even accent it with a scarf and a pair of heels," said Sasha.

"That would be nice, but I don't know where we're going, and I want to make sure I'm dressed for the occasion," said Jade. "So, I was thinking a simple cocktail dress would be perfect," she added, while searching through the new dress selection.

"I like this one," said Zoe as she held up a sexy, white chiffon dress.

"Let me see that one," said Jade, reaching for the dress. "This is the one I'm wearing. It's simple, yet sexy. Zoe, will you come ring me up?"

"Ring me up too, Zoe. I need to get going, ladies. It's been fun, but I have a charity event to prepare for. You should be receiving your tickets this week," Lola added. "I count on having all y'all's support, so I know I'll see you there, right?"

"You know we'll be there to support your organization," answered Jade.

"Yeah, you're doing a good thing by raising money for the less fortunate, and we want to be a part of it," said Sasha.

"Thanks, ladies. So, I'll see you there," said Lola as she walked out the door.

Zoe looked at the time. "Jade, are you still going to your aerobics class? If so, you should get going," said Zoe.

"Oh, no, what time is it?" asked Jade as she quickly ran to grab her gym bag from the back.

"It's 5 o'clock," said Sasha.

"You're right. I do need to get going," said Jade as she headed to the door. "Maybe I'll go along with you next time," yelled Zoe.

"Hey, do some squats for me," said Sasha. Jade and Zoe laughed.

"Have a good night!" Jade yelled as she walked out the door.

"Girly, you know, you should be going with her," said Sasha jokingly while walking over to straighten out the accessories table.

"You too," replied Zoe. Then they both looked at each other and giggled.

It was Thursday, and Jade prepared for her date with Tony. "Well, look at you," said Zoe as Jade walked in the boutique from her salon appointment. It was Thursday, and Jade prepared for her date with Tony.

"Hey, Zoe, how's everything?" asked Jade.

"Everything's fine around here, but let's check you out! Your hair and makeup look really nice," said Zoe, and she touched one of Jade's curls.

"Thanks," Jade replied. "So, where's Sasha?" she asked, laying her purse down.

"Oh, she's on her way," answered Zoe. "So, are you ready for your date tonight?"

"I sure am," Jade answered.

"Tony seems like a real gentleman," said Zoe. "It's nice when a man sends you flowers. It shows he has a bit of class."

"Yeah, it does," said Jade.

"I can't wait to meet this Tony," said Zoe.

"Soon enough," replied Jade, then she peeked through the window at the people walking by. "Well, look what the wind blew in."

"Hey, girlies," said Sasha, and she pranced in the boutique.

"Where have you been?" asked Jade. "Tony will be here in less than an hour," she added.

"Calm down... I'm here now," replied Sasha. "So, where's the dress you're wearing tonight?"

"Oh, it's hanging in the fitting room," Jade answered. "I'll go put it on," she added and laid her shades on the counter. Jade quickly went into the fitting room and closed the door behind her.

"By the way, your hair looks good. Miss Niecy really did her thing on you," said Sasha.

"Thanks. Yes, she does good work!" yelled Jade. "Can one of you come zip me up?" asked Jade as she stepped out of the fitting room. Zoe rushed over to help her.

"Wow, girly, you're looking all classy and stuff. You tell Tony to keep his hands to himself tonight," said Sasha as she teased Jade.

"Oh, hush..." Jade replied.

"You look very nice," said Zoe.

"Thank you both for your help. What would I do without you two?" Jade smiled.

"Hmm... we don't know!" answered Sasha. They all laughed. Suddenly, the boutique's phone rang.

"I'll get it," said Zoe, and she walked over to answer the call. "Hello. Chic Couture."

"Good evening. Is Jade available, please?"

"May I tell her who's calling?" asked Zoe.

"Sure, you can tell her it's Tony."

"One moment, please," said Zoe. "Jade, it's Tony," she whispered. Jade grabbed the phone from Zoe. "This is Jade."

"Hello, my sweet lady. I just wanted to tell you I'll be there to pick you up in two minutes," said Tony.

"Okay, I'll see you in a few," said Jade. They hung up the phone.

"What did he say?" asked Sasha.

"That he'll be here in two minutes," replied Jade.

"Well, we need to do the finishing touches," said Zoe as she helped Jade put on her necklace.

"Girly, those are some bad shoes you have on. I'm going to have to come borrow them one day," said Sasha.

"As long as I can borrow that silver-sequined purse I love so much," Jade replied.

"Hey, looks like a black limousine just pulled up in front of the door," said

Sasha.

"That must be him," replied Jade. "Okay, how do I look?"

"You look fine," answered Zoe.

"Yeah… you look fine, but he looks fine too," said Sasha.

"Let me see," said Zoe, and she peeked through the window with Sasha. "So, that's Tony? He is attractive."

"Look, here he comes," said Sasha as they quickly moved away from

the window.

"Good evening, ladies. I'm here to pick up Jade," he said politely.

"Hi, Tony. I'm ready. Let me just grab my purse," said Jade. "Oh, by the way, you remember Sasha, right?"

"I do—Mike's lady, and who might this be?" he asked.

"I'm Zoe, a friend of Jade's also."

"Nice meeting you," said Tony, and he reached to shake her hand. "Likewise," Zoe replied.

"So, how's business going in the big city?" asked Tony.

"It's going well," answered Sasha. "We were just asked to be featured in one of New York's most popular fashion magazines."

"Really? That's impressive," said Tony. "Congratulations to you all for running such a classy place," he added.

"Thank you," they all replied.

"So, how's your business doing?" asked Sasha.

"All is good," Tony replied. "Well, my sweet lady, are you ready? I have something really special awaiting our arrival."

"Yes, I guess we should be going then," answered Jade.

"Have a good night, ladies," said Tony. Jade smiled and waved bye to Zoe and Sasha.

"Ooohh... girly, did you hear that? Something awaiting their arrival, huh?" Sasha chuckled.

"I heard it," answered Zoe.

"I wonder what he has planned for them tonight," wondered Sasha.

"I don't know, but it sounds really special," replied Zoe.

"Well, look at the time! We should wrap it up here," Sasha said. "I have people to see and places to be."

Zoe laughed, "You always have something going on."

Jade and Tony arrived at their destination. "So, my sweet lady, how do you feel about big boats?" asked Tony. He surprisingly drove into a parking lot at the pier where there were large boats docked.

"I think they're nice," Jade replied. "Why do you ask?"

"Well, let me show you," said Tony as he walked around to open her door. He then took her hand and walked her to a beautiful blue and white yacht with the name 'Queen' painted on the side.

"This is really nice, but I thought we were going to dinner," said Jade.

"We are," he said softly. He pulled a red rose from behind his back and handed it to her.

Oh, my God, this man is so romantic, Jade thought to herself. "For me?" she asked.

"Yes, my sweet lady, for you," Tony replied with a smile.

"Is this your yacht?" asked Jade.

"It is," he answered. "Let me show you around." He then took her to the upper deck where everything was controlled. When they approached the top, Jade noticed a man and lady standing near the steering wheel.

"Hello, Captain Dave! Hello, Mrs. Dixon! This is Jade, the beautiful woman I was telling you about. She will be joining me for dinner this evening," said Tony.

"Wonderful," Mrs. Dixon replied. "Dinner will be in ready in a few minutes."

Jade looked at Tony and smiled, "What a nice surprise. I've never had dinner on a private boat before."

"Jade, my sweet lady, I wanted this night to be really special, so I thought we could have dinner here on my yacht."

"Nice choice," said Jade. Then she began looking around at how clean it was.

"Oh, by the way, Dave is actually the caretaker of my boat when I'm out of town on business, and his wife always comes out to help him. The Dixons are like family to me and have been for some years now," he explained. "The lovely Mrs. Dixon happened to own a small catering business in Midtown and is one fine cook, I must say. After telling them I was taking a beautiful young lady on a date, Mrs. Dixon insisted on having her company cater our dinner tonight."

Jade gazed out at the still water while Tony was talking. "It's a lovely night to have dinner outside, especially on the water. It's so romantic, and the setting reminds me of a painting I saw in the art gallery," she said.

"I'm glad you're enjoying yourself. I was hoping you would," said Tony.

Mrs. Dixon walked on the main deck where the two of them were standing. "Here you are. I thought you two may like something to drink while you wait for dinner," she said and handed them both a glass of red wine.

"Thank you," said Jade.

"You're welcome, dear," Mrs. Dixon replied. "Enjoy," she said before going back down to the lower level.

"That Mrs. Dixon is something else," said Tony as he took a sip from his glass.

"They seem like a really sweet couple," said Jade.

"Yeah, Dave sure does miss her when she's not working with him on the yacht," said Tony.

"Aww... How nice two love birds that can't get enough of each other," Jade said with a smile.

"Dinner is ready!" yelled Mrs. Dixon from the lower deck. Tony took Jade by the hand and helped her down the stairs.

"Wow, the ambience is so beautiful," she said while admiring the lighting, the plush, red carpet, and the elegant table set up for them.

"Here, let me get that for you," said Tony and pulled her chair out for her sit.

"Thank you," said Jade as she took her seat.

"You're welcome, my sweet lady," replied Tony.

"Dinner is now being served," said Mrs. Dixon before heading back upstairs, "and this fine gentleman will take it from here."

A man dressed in a tuxedo walked up and began pouring water into their empty glasses. "I hope you'll enjoy tonight's special: shrimp linguine alfredo." He then grabbed two plates from a steel cart beside him and placed them in front of them.

"This is my favorite pasta dish," said Jade, looking up at the waiter then at Tony.

"Enjoy, ma'am," said the waiter and walked away, leaving the two of them alone.

"How did you know what to put on the menu?" asked Jade as she looked at Tony with her big, brown eyes, which is what he remembered the first time they met.

"A man truly interested in a woman never forgets what she likes," he answered.

Jade blushed and placed her napkin in her lap, then looked up only to see Tony reaching his hands toward hers.

"It's been a while since I've done this, so please don't laugh at me," he said. Jade smiled, then they both bowed their heads for a short and sweet prayer.

"That was good," she said. "It seems like this is something you really know how to do."

"Yeah, I do, but it slipped away from me somehow," he answered.

"Really? Why did you allow such a beautiful thing, such as prayer, to get away from you?" she asked.

"Oh, I pray, and I talk to the Big Fella—just not over my food all the time."

"Ah, I see," Jade replied.

"Yeah, you know how it is when you are moving quick, and it kind of slips your mind," Tony answered.

"Yes, I understand, but you should try getting back on that track."

"Thanks, my sweet lady. I agree and will try and do better with that," Tony added. "Gratitude is very important. Just as I'm thankful you're here and for this meal, which is why we should start eating before it gets cold. I don't like cold food that should be hot."

Jade giggled. "I agree," she said.

"Umm... This is delicious," said Tony. "I see why this is a favorite of yours. It's really good."

"Yes, it is. Glad you like it, too," said Jade.

"So, I hear you were chosen to be featured in a magazine. That's great news. Congratulations," said Tony.

"Thank you! It was a real surprise to the ladies and me."

"I'm sure it was," he replied.

"Well, what about you? How's everything going with you and Mike at the firm?" asked Jade.

"It's going well. Mike is my right-hand man, although I must admit, he doesn't know anything about my side business yet. I work at the firm because I enjoy it—not because I have to. Plus, I like my team, and we work really well together. We've been talking about taking a business trip, but a date hasn't been set yet," Tony added.

"That should be exciting," said Jade.

"Yeah, business meetings are usually a win for me. Well, for us," Tony replied. "So, do you have children?"

"I do," answered Jade. "What about you?"

"Yes, I have a son and a daughter," he answered.

"So, do I! Wow, that's interesting."

"Yes, it is," said Tony.

"So, where are they now?" asked Jade.

"They're in Atlanta with their mother. Are your kids at a sitter's tonight?" asked Tony.

"No, they're with their dad for the summer," she answered.

"Oh, I see. That must give you a break, huh?"

"Yes, it does, but I really miss them when they're away. They're my blessings," said Jade smiling.

"I understand. You're a mother, and I can tell you're a really good one," said Tony.

"Thank you," she replied and took a sip of her water. Jade then glanced out the small window near their table. "So, do you see your kids often?"

"Not as often as I would like, but we do keep in touch. I try to visit them when I can, and they come up here from time to time," he answered.

"That's good. Sounds like you try to be a good dad."

"Oh, yeah, I'm very supportive of them. They're my little troopers," replied Tony.

Jade smiled. He then got up from the table and turned on some soft jazz music. "May I have this dance?" he asked and helped her up from the seat.

"Yes, you may," she answered and held his hand.

After they walked out into the center of the room, Tony lightly embraced Jade, and they started moving to the music. "This is nice," said Tony.

"What is?" asked Jade, lifting her head from his shoulder.

"Me dancing here with the most beautiful woman I ever laid eyes on," he answered.

Jade blushed. "Oh," she said, looking into his dark brown eyes.

"You are one fine woman, Jade," he complimented and placed a kiss on her hand.

"You're one fine man, Mr. Jacobs," replied Jade and placed her arms around his neck.

"The night is still young," he said. "How about I take you to the upper deck, so you can show me that view you were admiring earlier?"

"I would like that," Jade answered. Then she grabbed her purse from the back of the chair and headed up the stairs. "Where are the Dixons?" asked Jade.

"Probably up in the captain's suite," he answered.

"This is a nice yacht you have here," said Jade and looked around the upper deck.

"Thank you, my sweet lady," he replied.

"This is the view that I was admiring earlier," Jade said and walked over to the rail. Tony grabbed her hand as they both looked up at the stars and the moon in the sky. "This is so peaceful," she said. "I don't remember when I had such a lovely evening," Jade added and turned toward Tony. "Thank you," she said while gazing in his eyes.

"You're so welcome, my sweet lady, and you deserve so much more," he said leaning forward to kiss her cheek.

"Well, it's getting late, and I should be going now," said Jade, shying away from him.

"Okay, let me tell them we're leaving and to lock up for me," he replied.

"I'll wait here," said Jade, and she sat down on the couch looking out at the water.

After a few minutes passed, Tony came back to find Jade enjoying the city's view, reminiscing about their lovely evening. "I'm ready, my sweet lady," he said softly then helped her up off the couch. When she stood up, they caught each other's eyes again and gazed at one another for a few seconds. Tony then slowly leaned in and kissed her lips. Suddenly, Jade's eyes were closed as she embraced the moment. "Thank you for a lovely evening," Tony said after slowly moving back from her.

Jade smiled then draped her shawl across her shoulders. "I don't usually kiss on the first date."

"Yeah, I haven't done that in a long time myself," replied Tony. Then they walked off the yacht holding hands like two people in love.

3

"Hey," Lola said to Jade as she, Zoe, and Sasha entered the convention center where the 5th Annual Charity Fashion Show was being held.

"Ladies, you made it!" Lola excitedly said, greeting them with a hug and side kiss like they do in France.

"Girly, we wouldn't miss this for the world," said Sasha.

"Yeah, that's right, and plus, I want to see what celebrities are going to be here tonight," said Zoe. Jade smiled and checked out the decorations in the lobby.

"Make yourselves at home. Y'all are my special guests this evening," said Lola. Then she quickly rushed over to greet some of the other guests as they arrived.

"Come on... let's find our seats," said Jade.

"Wow! It's really crowded," said Sasha, looking around to see all the other guests already in the auditorium.

"Look! There's what's-his-name," yelled Zoe.

"Who?" asked Jade.

"I don't remember his name, but he's the designer of that popular Italian shoe line that everyone's buying."

"Oh, yeah, that is him," said Sasha.

"Where?" asked Jade.

"Right there, behind that lady with the bad hairdo," answered Zoe. Jade and Sasha both looked at Zoe and shook their heads, then they laughed.

"Come on. Let's take our seats. The fashion show is about to begin," said Jade. The three sat down next to the two ladies that came into the boutique earlier in the week.

"Well, hello again," said Kim as she noticed Jade sitting beside her.

"I didn't know you would be here tonight," said Kori.

"Yes, our friend is the hostess of this event," answered Jade.

"Oh, so you know Lola?" asked Kim.

"I do...She's also one of my most faithful customers. She's wearing one of our newest arrivals tonight," said Jade.

"We were wondering where she got that beautiful dress," said Kim.

"I knew we made a good decision by choosing Chic Couture to be in our next issue. You ladies have style," said Kori.

"Thank you," replied Jade. Sasha and Zoe remained quiet as they waited for the show to begin.

"Listen! Lola's about to introduce the first model," said Sasha as the lights began to dim.

"She really looks nice up there," said Zoe.

"Yes, she does," said Jade.

"Now is this charity event hosted every year for the same cause, or do they give money to other charities?" asked Kori.

"Every year they raise money for the same cause," answered Jade, overhearing Kori's question.

"Oh, that's sweet," said Kori. "I always wanted to find a good organization to partner with, so that I can become a sponsor. I truly believe in giving back and helping the less fortunate," Kori added.

"Well, this is a good place to start," said Jade. "Lola has been doing this for a few years and is always in need of some new sponsors."

"Thank you. I'll keep that in mind," replied Kori.

"Oooh... check out that suit that girl is wearing. It almost looks like one of ours," said Sasha.

"It is one of ours!" Jade and Zoe both yelled softly.

"That's one of the outfits we donated," said Jade.

"Oh, well, it looks really nice on," replied Sasha.

"You ladies donated some outfits from the boutique?" asked Kim.

"We definitely need to add that in our article under the 'Chic Couture: Heart and Style' section," Kim added.

"Yes, we've been donating items from the boutique for a couple of years now. Lola is such a nice person, and we look forward to supporting this event every year," said Jade.

"I see," replied Kim. Then she took out a small pad and began writing.

"Now, check out this bald, handsome, brown sugar coming down the runway," said Kori.

"Oooh...my Mikey would look good in that," said Sasha.

"That does look nice on him. I see some of the men are writing that one down," said Jade.

"Oh, but I wasn't talking about what he was wearing. I was talking about him," said Kori. They all looked at her and smiled. "Hey, I'm still single," Kori whispered. "I don't know about y'all." They all covered their mouths and giggled.

Well, it was towards the end of the show. As Lola said her closing remarks, everyone stood and clapped, and then they started walking toward the lobby. "Ladies!" yelled Lola while trying to catch up with Jade, Sasha, and Zoe, "Thanks for coming out tonight and supporting my organization."

"You're welcome," replied Jade.

"Yeah, girly, you're welcome," said Sasha, and she gave Lola a hug. Then she went over to peek outside at all the limousines lined up.

"Ladies, thank you also for coming out tonight," said Lola as she extended her arm to shake hands with Kim and Kori.

"You're welcome, Lola, and thanks for the invitation. It was a nice show, so we definitely look forward to next year's event," said Kim.

"Well, Kim, Kori, it was nice seeing you again, and we look forward to our interview next week," said Jade.

"Okay, y'all have a good night," said Kim.

"Yes, goodnight, ladies, and we will see you next week," Kori added.

"Come on, we should be going now. I have a meeting with a buyer in the morning," said Jade.

"Wait, where's Sasha?" asked Zoe.

"Oh, she's outside checking out the sites. You know how she is," said Jade. They both smiled and walked outside to get Sasha.

Jade then headed home. Upon entering her building, "Hello, Mr. Franklin."

"Well, hello there, Ms. Taylor. How have you been these days?"

"I've been doing well. Just got back from a charity event that a friend of mine hosted at the convention center downtown," Jade replied.

"Oh, that's nice. You ladies sure stick together I see. By the way, how's that friend of yours doing, the one that's always talking?" he asked.

"Who? Sasha? She's doing well. I just left her and Zoe at the convention," answered Jade. "Well, have a good night, Mr. Franklin. I need to get up there to check on our puppy."

Mr. Franklin smiled. "Goodnight, Ms. Taylor."

"Hey, Skittles, I'm home!" said Jade after entering her condo and picking her up. She walked over to the fridge, grabbed a bottled water, kicked off her shoes, and flopped down on her couch. "It's been a long day," she said rubbing the top of Skittles' head.

Jade decided to take out her cell phone to call Tony. Suddenly, she changed her mind and laid the phone down on the countertop. Hesitantly, she picked it back up again. *Should I call him?* she questioned herself. *No, he's probably busy.* Jade placed the phone on the bed after walking in her bedroom. *I'm just going to shower, do a little reading, and go to bed.*

The phone rang while Jade was flipping through pages of a magazine.

"Hello?" she said, answering the call.

"Hi, Mommy!" said Brittany.

"Hi, baby, how are y'all doing?" asked Jade.

"We miss you, Mommy, but we're good," replied Brittany.

"Glad to hear it, and I'm even more happy to hear from you," Jade said. "So, where's your brother, and why haven't you called me sooner?"

"Oh, Mommy, we've only been gone a couple of weeks," said Brittany.

"I know, baby! Mommy just misses y'all, that's all."

"Mommy, how's Skittles doing?"

"She's fine. I'll tell her you said hi. Okay?"

"Okay. Kiss her for me, too, please," Brittany added.

Jade smiled. "I heard you, baby. Now, let me talk to Jayden."

"Okay, Mommy, hold on so I can get him for you," she said.

"Brittany!" Jade yelled.

"Yes, Mommy?" she answered.

"I love you," said Jade.

"Love you, too, Mommy. Now hold please."

"Jayden! Mommy's on the phone and wants to talk to you."

"Wow, that girl has some lungs on her," Jade mumbled as she waited for Jayden to pick up the phone.

"Hi, Mom!" said Jayden.

"Hey, how's my little man?" she asked.

"I'm fine, Mom. We're having lots of fun with Dad, Grandma, and Grandpa."

"That's good, honey. I'm having fun, too, with Auntie Sasha and Ms. Zoe," said Jade and chuckled. Jayden chuckled also. "So, where's your dad?" asked Jade.

"He ran to the store to get us some ice cream," he answered.

"Umm... that sounds yummy," replied Jade.

"Well, Mom, I was watching my favorite TV show, so can I call you back when it goes off ?" asked Jayden.

"No, that's okay. Mommy just wanted to hear your voice."

"Oh, well, I love you, Mom."

"I love you, too, and enjoy your ice cream," said Jade. She put the phone on her nightstand, and then she looked at the clock. *My... it's getting late,* she thought and laid back on the bed.

I wonder what Tony's doing, Jade thought. *He's probably asleep by now with his fine, sexy self. Oooh ... look at me. I should be going to bed myself.* Then the phone rang. *I wonder who this is?* She reached for her phone to answer the call. "Hello?" said Jade.

"Hello, lovely lady. This is Tony."

"Hi, Tony," she said, covering the phone and smiling with excitement. "Is this a good time for you to talk?" he asked.

"Sure, I was just thinking about you," replied Jade.

"Really? I was just thinking about you, too, and how I can't wait to see that beautiful face of yours again," said Tony. "So, how about I treat you to a cup of coffee in the morning?"

"That would nice. We can meet at the coffee shop on Broadway," said Jade. "What time would you like me to be there?" asked Tony.

"How about 9?"

"I'll be there. Well, lovely lady, I just wanted to hear your voice before I turn in. Plus, you need to rest those pretty eyes of yours. I know how you ladies like to get your beauty sleep."

After a soft chuckle, Jade replied, "Yes, we do. You do that, and I'll just look forward to seeing your gorgeous face in the morning. Have a good night, Tony."

"Sweet dreams," he replied.

It was the next day, and after having breakfast with Tony, Jade was off to her interview session at *Style Magazine* on 21st Street. Jade walked through the glass double doors and up the escalators. She was sophisticated dressed in a black knee-length pencil skirt, a white silk blouse, a red "top of the line" Italian leather handbag, red pumps, and black sunshades.

Who is she? Jade overheard the whispering in the background, which she was used to getting when she walked into a room. The stares and the curiosity were nothing new to her. She just smiled and strutted on. Jade approached the reception desk. The young lady confirmed her appointment with Kim and escorted Jade to her office. "Right this way, Ms. Taylor," she politely said. She opened a set of cherry wood doors that led to a beautiful, large office with a gorgeous view of the city. "Kim will be right with you," said the receptionist before closing the doors behind her, leaving Jade alone in the office. Jade laid her purse on the table and went to look out the big window.

"Ms. Taylor, how are you this morning?" asked Kim, rushing in with a coffee mug, mini recorder, pen, and a pad.

"I'm doing well, and thanks again for choosing our boutique to be featured in your next issue," replied Jade as she turned to shake her hand.

"You're welcome! We're just glad you agreed to meet with us. Oh, I'm sorry. Did you want anything before we get started?" Kim asked while taking a sip of her coffee.

"Well...some water would be good," Jade answered.

Kim then buzzed the receptionist. "Jasmine, can you please get Ms. Taylor some water?"

"Sure," she answered.

"Thank you. Okay... Now, where do you want to begin?" asked Kim.

"How about I tell you how we got started, and then we'll go into the merchandise and styles that we carry?"

"Wow, you're a natural! Sounds good to me," Kim replied. She pushed record on her mini recorder. "Today, I am interviewing Ms. Jade Taylor, the manager of Chic Couture Clothing Boutique in the heart of downtown Manhattan. She's going to be sharing with us how she got started in the industry—the business and fashion side of it all. We will also be talking a little about Jade's personal life if that's okay with her," said Kim and peeked over at Jade to see her facial reaction.

Jade began telling her all about the boutique and how she got started in the industry. They were about an hour into the meeting when Kim began wrapping up the interview. "Well, Jade, that's it. We're done here," she said. "I wish you much success in the near future. In addition, I will pass the word on of where to buy some of New York's most fashionable garments and accessories," Kim added.

"Thank you. It has been my pleasure speaking with you today, and I look forward to reading next month's issue of *Style*," replied Jade.

Jade left their office. She took out her cell phone to call the boutique. The phone rang. "Hey Sasha. The interview went well, and I'm about to grab a bite to eat. I was wondering if you wanted to join me for lunch. We can check out that new café on the corner of 23rd Street."

"Sure, girly. I'll meet you there around one o'clock. You know my saying, 'If you're treatin', I'm eatin'," replied Sasha.

Jade laughed. "Bye…," she said and hung up the phone.

As Jade walked to the parking lot, a text message came through that read: *It was so nice seeing you this morning. I wish it didn't have to end. I want to spend more time with you... How soon can we begin?*

Jade blushed. "Lord...that man has all the right words," she said softly. Then she quickly responded with: *Let's begin with you coming over to dinner this evening.*

Tony then replied with a smiley face and the words*: Lovely lady that you are. I'd rather be close than afar, so I accept your invitation to be in the presence of such a beauty.* Jade smiled as she read his response. "Oooh... I love his wording."

Then she replied: *Dinner at eight. My place, and don't be late because I don't want to wait to spend this time with such a handsome date.* Jade included her address, hit the send button, and put her phone in her purse.

"Oh, my, let me hurry up. Sasha's probably on her way," Jade said then got into the car and drove off. She turned up the music on her stereo and let the window down to feel the breeze blowing.

"Hey, that's my song!" Jade yelled while nodding her head to the beat. *I wonder what I'm going to make for dinner tonight,* she thought. *Well, whatever I come up with has to be special because he's special.* Jade then took her cell phone out her purse and noticed she had a missed call. *Humm... I don't recognize this number. I wonder who that was,* she thought. *It's an out-of-state number too.*

"Wait a minute! That call was from Mexico!" Jade yelled in disbelief as she looked closely at the digits. *Who in the world would be calling me from Mexico? I know Mama and Papa didn't take a trip and not tell me.* She pondered again. *I know it's not any of my friends and definitely not my brother. So, who's left? Oh, well, they didn't leave a message. So, I won't worry about it.*

Jade arrived in front of the café. "Alright, I'm here, and I don't see Sasha's car," Jade mumbled as she pulled in front of the jewelry store next to the café. "I guess Sasha's running late, as usual," she said and shook her head.

Just as Jade stepped out the car, she saw good ole Mr. Walker. He was sweeping the front step of the jewelry store. "Hello there, Mr. Walker!"

"Hi there, Ms. Jade," he replied while watching her walk past. "If only I was a little younger…," Mr. Walker said then wiped his forehead and continued sweeping.

Meanwhile, Jade decided to take a seat in the café until Sasha arrived. She gazed out the window in deep thought about the call that was missed earlier. Sasha walked up behind Jade.

"Hey, girly, sorry I'm late," she said quietly.

"Oh, hey," Jade replied with discontent in her voice.

"My goodness, what's wrong with you?" Sasha asked.

"Oh, nothing," Jade replied and gazed back out the window.

"Yeah, right. You're talking to your best friend here," said Sasha while moving her hand from her face.

"Okay, I had a missed call a little while ago, and I don't know who it was from."

"Big deal. I get that all the time," Sasha replied then looked around for a waiter. "Don't even worry about it," she added.

"I wouldn't normally, but I have this funny feeling it's from Blaine," Jade expressed with wondering thoughts.

"Really, chica? Blaine?" Sasha said and put her purse down. She scooted her chair up to the table to give Jade her full attention.

"Yes!" Jade answered quickly.

"Why would he be calling you now?" asked Sasha.

"From Mexico at that!" Jade added.

"Wow... Mexico? Well, did he leave a message?" asked Sasha.

"No. I didn't see that I had any voice messages."

"Okay, so, don't worry about it, and let's get something to eat now because I'm starving," said Sasha. She then began to read over the menu.

"Yeah, you're right. I'm not going to make a big deal over a call that was probably a mistake anyway," Jade replied and began looking at the menu also.

"So, girly, tell me about you and Mr. Bling," said Sasha teasingly.

"Stop calling him that! He's a good man, and I really like him," Jade replied.

"Alright, I won't call him that anymore," said Sasha as she smiled and looked out the window.

"Anyway, Tony and I are having dinner at my house tonight, and yes, I'm cooking for him," said Jade.

"You go, girly! So, how was your date that night he picked you up from the boutique?" asked Sasha.

"Oh, my God. It was wonderful...... He took me to his yacht on the harbor, and we had a beautiful dinner. Tony really out did himself that night," Jade replied while reminiscing about their evening together.

"Girly, he out does himself every time from what I've seen so far. I must admit: You may have found your Mr. Right," said Sasha. "He's clearly into you and shows it. You know that's what all women want to have in their relationship: a good man that shows his love for you," Sasha added and sipped some of her water.

"Yeah, he is good, but we will see as time goes on," Jade responded then dropped a lemon in her water and began sipping it.

"I know you don't want to get hurt, and that's totally understandable." Sasha expressed her feelings as she thought of her past. "Been there," she added.

"Yes, you're right. I don't. I'm so hoping he's the one. I don't want to find out something later that could mess things up," Jade replied.

"Well, he better not mess up, or he'll have me to deal with!" replied Sasha. "You know your girls got your back."

"Oh, yeah, I know that all too well," Jade said and thought back a few years ago. "Wait a minute!" Jade quickly shifted tones as she put her glass down on the table. "Did Ms. Sasha just get all sentimental on me or what?"

"Huh—Who? Me? No, not I," Sasha replied and took a bite of the turkey sandwich she ordered. They both laughed and began eating. Jade decided to go with a salad since she and Tony were having dinner later that evening. "Umm, this is really good," Sasha said then wiped her mouth.

"Yeah, my salad is good, too, but they could have put a little more chicken in it," Jade replied.

"This is a café—not a bistro," said Sasha, shaking her head.

"Oh, never mind," Jade said and mixed her salad and dressing together before eating more.

"So, back to your date on Tony's yacht: How was the service?" Sasha asked. "Because I know he had it!"

Laughing, Jade shook her head, "Yes, he did have servers, which happened to be the employees of the captain's wife. She owns a catering company."

"Captain?" Sasha questioned.

"Oh, yeah, the captain of his yacht was there, of course, and he brought his wife along. They are such a friendly couple and were very welcoming. Tony explained that they're like his family and have been for a long time now," Jade explained.

"That's nice, girly. Glad you had a good time. Maybe Tony will invite your friends out on his yacht one day," Sasha said excitedly.

"Yes, maybe," Jade responded and began wrapping things up so she could leave. "Okay, I need to get going. I have some things to pick up from the grocery store."

"Oh, yeah, that's right. You are cooking dinner tonight. Does Mama know?" Sasha asked, referring to Jade's mother.

"No, she doesn't even know that I'm having dinner with Tony. We haven't had the conversation about him yet," Jade added then stood up to fix her clothes.

"Oh, well, I wouldn't worry her, and Papa will love him, especially knowing that he's a good guy," said Sasha.

"Yeah, I hope you're right," Jade replied. "No one is good enough for Papa's J."

"True," Sasha agreed. They both smiled. Jade left the tab on the table, and they both walked out. "Hey, girly, are you going to be in church on this Sunday?" Sasha asked. "You know, they invited that handsome guest preacher from Atlanta, and the mass choir is singing," she added as they headed out the door."

"Most definitely. I have to get the Word. That's what keeps me going," Jade replied then gave Sasha a hug. "Hmmm, what are you going for?" Jade jokingly asked.

"The Word, girly. What else?"

"Hmm… I hope so," Jade said.

"It is, and I was thinking about bringing Mike along," replied Sasha.

"That would be really nice," said Jade.

Sasha waved her hand and kept walking. "Okay, see you Sunday, and I'll be waiting to hear all about your dinner date with Mr. Bling."

Jade gave Sasha a funny look. "Just kidding! Bye, girly! Love ya," said Sasha jokingly.

"Love ya, too, and tell Zoe I'll call her about the new signage for the boutique," said Jade.

"Will do, and you tell Brittany and Jayden that I said, 'Hello and Auntie misses them'," Sasha said as they departed to their vehicles.

Jade headed the grocery store. She grabbed a small cart and thought, *Okay, what do I need? Hmm… I'll definitely need this.* She picked up a loaf of freshly baked Italian bread then placed it in her cart. *Well, since I'm making lasagna, I would want to have salad with it,* she thought and turned down the produce aisle.

There, she saw, standing in the fruit section, a chocolate-delight-of-a-man, wearing gray basketball shorts, a white t-shirt, and some sneakers. He was at least 6'1 or 6'2, but just the way she likes 'em. *Aww… I think it's so cute to see a guy shopping for his own groceries,* Jade thought while moving a little closer, so she could get what she needed.

Jade continued to admire from a distance. The man then placed a bag of grapes in his cart and looked over to notice Jade watching. She smiled and quickly turned her head the other way. "Wow! He has some nice legs," she softly said and walked away. "Uhmm, and young too."

After seeing Jade and finding her to be very attractive, the man remembered seeing her somewhere, but couldn't remember where. Then it hit him. "Excuse me!" he yelled, just enough for her to hear him. "Is your name Ms. Taylor?" he asked.

"Yes, it is, and you are?" she questioned while looking surprised that he knew her name.

"I'm Coach Brooks—to the kids that is," he answered.

"Oh, well, nice to meet you, Mr. Brooks," Jade replied, wondering if they had met before.

"No, call me Orlando."

"Okay, Orlando. You can call me Jade," she replied. "So, how is it that you know me, and I don't know you?" she then asked.

"I see you around the school from time-to-time. I'm going to be the new coach for your son's basketball team. I just started this year, and I have already heard so much about him," Orlando said.

"Oh, really? Well, that's wonderful!" she replied. "He's a good player, and as any mom would say, I want my son to be the best that he can be."

"I know you do, and I will do all that I can to help make that happen," he gladly replied.

"Thanks," she said and slowly started walking again. Orlando quickly followed behind to catch up with her.

"So, I also hear his dad is a professional ball player," he said and dropped a bag of cookies in his cart.

"Yes, I guess you could say that," she answered. "That's where he is now," Jade replied while struggling to put a case of water in her cart.

"Hey, let me help you with that," said Orlando and took the case of water from Jade's hands.

"Why, thank you. That was really kind," she said.

"Well, my mom did raise me right and taught me to always be a gentleman to the ladies," he boldly replied.

"Sounds like you have yourself a good mom."

"Oh, yeah, no doubt about that, and from the sound of it, Jayden has himself a good one also," he said with a smile. *Not to mention drop dead gorgeous*, he thought to himself.

Jade then smiled and placed a few more items in her cart. "Well, it was really nice meeting you today, but I must be going now. I believe I have everything that I came for and a little more," she said then chuckled. "So, you take care, and I look forward to seeing you at the games," she added and quickly headed to the register.

"Yeah! Me too!" he yelled. "Hey, maybe we can…" Before he could finish, Jade walked off. "Have dinner together sometime?" Orlando softly mumbled under his breath.

Jade stuck the keys in her condo door, and before she could open it, Skittles started to bark. "Hi, Skittles! What's all the fuss about?" asked Jade, and she walked in the kitchen to place her groceries on the counter. "You must be glad to see me. Well, I miss you too," Jade added while bending down to pet Skittles' head.

Jade then walked in her bedroom to change her clothes. She opened her dresser drawer and held up an old pair of blue jeans, Daisy Duke shorts. She pulled a white tank top from her top shelf. *This will do,* Jade thought and slipped the tank over her head.

She peeked at her answering machine to see if the light was blinking. "Good. No messages," said Jade and went back into the kitchen to prepare dinner. "Okay, where should I start?" she questioned and pulled her hair up into a ponytail.

Jade decided to grab a pot out of the cabinet to boil some water for the noodles. "Homemade lasagna…Wow! I must really like him," she said excitedly then paused for a moment and thought back at his gorgeous smile. "Yeah… he's worth it."

The phonc rang soon after Jade got everything ready. "Who might this be?" she questioned after laying the cutting knife down and quickly running over to answer the call. "Oh, it's Mama! Hi, Mom," she said after picking up her cell phone to see who it was.

"Hello, J! How's Mama's businesswoman doing in the Big Apple?"

"I'm doing well, Mama, and the kids are fine too."

"That's good to hear, dear. So, what you up to on this beautiful evening the Lord done gave us?" Mama asked.

Jade smiled. "Well… I have a date tonight."

"You do? What's his name?"

"Tony," she answered with a smile.

"Where did you meet this Tony, and how long have you two been dating?" asked Mama.

"Okay, Mama, slow down with the questions, please. We have only been on a couple dates, but they have been the most amazing ones since you-know-who," replied Jade. "But to answer your question, we met at a restaurant. I was invited out by Sasha and Mike to a little dinner party," Jade explained.

"So, does he seem to be a good man, J?" Mama asked.

"Yes, he does, and I really like this one too," replied Jade.

"Okay, baby. Well, as long as you're happy, then alright," said Mama.

Jade held the phone away from her mouth and shook her head. "Gee… Thanks for your approval, Mama, but I am grown, remember?" she humbly said.

"I know, J. Mama just wants the best for her children as you want for yours."

"Yes, that is true, and again, thank you as always," replied Jade and cracked a little grin. "So, how's Papa been doing these days?"

"Oh, Papa's good! He's his usual self. Always working—that's all, but I do know he misses you and the kids too," Mama replied.

"Yeah, we miss y'all also. It's just that I've been so busy with Jayden's basketball games, Brittany's dance classes, and working at the boutique."

"We understand, baby," Mama said calmly. "You're trying to take care of those children without a dad in the home, and I know that's not an easy task. You do know your Papa and me are here anytime you need us… Right?"

"Yes, I do, and I also have the help of my friends here in New York," Jade answered.

Mama got silent for a few seconds. "Well, I know you have a date tonight, so I won't hold you any longer, dear. Oh, by the way, where is this Tony taking you?"

"Nowhere this time. I'm cooking for him," answered Jade excitedly.

"You're cooking? Really? My J is cooking? Wait until I tell Papa. He won't believe his ears," said Mama, laughing through the phone.

"Hey, what's so funny? I cook for the kids all the time. I may not be a chef, but I do pretty good, thanks to you and the food network channels. Hey, you know what? I'll tell Papa I'm cooking myself!" Jade said anxiously. "Where is he? Put me on speaker so Papa can hear me."

"Alright, alright, hold on one second," Mama said. "You know, I'm still learning how to work these fancy phones," she added.

Jade glanced at the time while waiting on Papa to come to the phone. "J, babe, you there?" asked Papa.

"Yes, I'm here," she answered.

"How's my baby girl?" he asked.

"I'm doing good, Papa," Jade answered.

"That's what I like to hear," he replied.

"Papa, I have something to tell you," she said. "I'm cooking dinner tonight for a manfriend of mine," Jade added as her voice lowered.

"Really?" Papa asked. "So, you done met someone out there, huh?"

"Yes, he's a guy I've been seeing for a little while now," she replied. "His name is Tony, and I really like him," Jade added then glanced at the time again.

"Well, J, if you like him, then I'm glad for you," said Papa. "He just better treat my baby girl right, so I don't have to put one across his head."

Jade laughed. "Oh… Papa, you are too much. Well, you two take care. I have to go now. I have a meal to prepare."

"Okay, baby, you go ahead but remember what I told you about men. Oh, and that good old saying, 'Love will come find you'," said Mama.

"I know, but I still have to make myself available if love is what I want," Jade replied. "Love is what I want, Mama, which is also the reason I took Sasha up on her invitation and went out with them that night. See what happened? I met a charming man who will be here shortly," she said.

"Yes, that's true, dear," said Mama, "but don't you be rushing into anything, and make sure that man treats you like the queen you are."

"Yes, ma'am," replied Jade. "I will also remember to tell Brittany the same when she gets older."

"Okay, baby, I'm going to let you finish your meal," said Mama, followed by a little chuckle. "Tell my grands I said, 'Hi and we love them.' "

"I will, Mama. Oh, have you heard anything from Zack?" asked Jade, wondering how her big brother was doing.

"Yes, just the other day. We talked briefly. But from the sound of it, he and the family are well."

"Good! Glad to hear it. Okay, well, let me finish cutting up my veggies," said Jade, rinsing off a piece of lettuce.

"Alright, dear, have yourself a good time tonight. I love you!" said Mama.

"Love y'all too!" Jade said. She hung up the phone and hurried to finish the salad. "Now, back to the drawing board," she joyfully said and continued her dinner preparation.

Time went by, and it got closer to Tony's arrival. "Now, here goes the fun part…" said Jade after a small sigh; then, she opened the door of her huge walk-in closet. "What will I wear for him?" she questioned, searching through a large clothes selection and tons of shoes. *Uhm… this is nice*, she thought, holding a purple short-sleeved, ruffled, off-the-shoulder dress up to her chest. "Nah…. this isn't it," she said and placed it back in the selection. "How about this?" Jade pulled out a tank-strapped, black mini. "Hmmm… sexy, but not for tonight. I need something very classy but tasteful," she said and continued her search. "Out of all these dresses, I can't find one that's right for this night," Jade mumbled as she began to get a little frustrated. "Hold on… this is it! This is the one!" She excitedly grabbed a black, modestly form-fitted midi dress with spaghetti straps, which stopped right above the knee and accented with a black patent belt around the waistline.

Now, for the shoes, Jade thought and reached up to pull down a sexy pair of leopard, peep-toe, five-inch platform heels from her shoe rack. "I love it!" she exclaimed then laid her dress on the bed. "I sure hope he loves it too," Jade then said while preparing herself for a shower. "Wow…

Look at the time! I need to make this a quick one."

After stepping into her gold-trimmed glass shower, she began humming her favorite song as the water streamed down her body. Meanwhile, a text message came through that read: *Have fun, and love ya, girly!*

… Sasha.

Skittles ran in the bedroom and started barking at the cell phone, which was laying on her bed. Jade overheard the loud noise and turned off the water to see what was wrong. She looked over and found

Skittles sitting next to the bed, staring at her phone. Jade then grabbed a towel to dry off.

"Mmmm… I hope that lasagna is as good as it smells," she said and lightly sniffed the aroma of green peppers and garlic simmering in tomato meat sauce which filled the air.

Then after picking up a bottle of her jasmine scented lotion, she began rubbing it all over her caramel colored skin. Before Jade put on her dress, she decided to read her text message. "Aww…" she said then smiled and tossed her phone back on the bed. *That Sasha*, she thought while picking up her dress and putting it on. *Good, it still fits!*

Jade happily sat on the stool to her vanity set, put on her heels, and checked herself in the mirror. *Cute!* With one hand on her hip, she did a little turn, struck a pose, and started giggling. She patted and picked at her hair; then she took out her makeup bag and began applying some lip gloss. Taking one last look in the mirror and blowing herself a kiss, she said, "Beautiful!"

Jade picked up one of her most expensive bottles of perfume. She sprayed it in the air, allowing the fragrance to fall on her. "Now, I'm ready!" she said and gracefully walked to the living room. "Now how about some music to set the mood?" She turned on some smooth jazz, swaying her hips side-to-side to the soft tunes.

Jade went in the kitchen. After washing her hands, she placed the food on the table, lit two cream colored candles, and dimmed her lights. Suddenly, the doorbell rang…

"Wow, just in time," said Jade and quickly walked over to the door. "Hello, Tony," she pleasantly said, opening the door. "Do come in."

"Hello to you, my lovely lady, and don't you look stunning tonight?" he said then placed a soft kiss on her cheek.

"Why, thank you, and might I say, you look rather handsome tonight, Mr. Jacobs. Umm… and you smell good too," she muttered under her breath.

He took a seat on her beige, Italian leather couch. "Ahh… this is nice," said Tony. Then he ran his hands across the arm of her couch, "And what a nice place you have here."

"Thanks," said Jade. Then she strutted into the kitchen to grab two wine glasses from the cabinet and returned to Tony. "May I pour you a glass of wine?" she asked, holding a bottle of pinot noir in one hand.

"Allow me," he said and got up to go over where Jade was standing.

"Oh, no, you're my guest. Plus, I would love to serve you. It will be my pleasure," she said and gazed into his eyes.

"I insist, and the pleasure is equally mine," said Tony and slowly took the bottle from her hand.

"You are such a gentleman."

"And you are such a lady," Tony flirtatiously replied.

"I know you have good taste in wine, so I bought this bottle of pinot noir. I hope you like it," said Jade.

Tony popped the cork. "I'm sure I will," he replied and poured Jade a glass first then one for himself. "Something sure smells good over here," he said and peeked around Jade's shoulder at the table.

"Thank you," she replied. "I did it all for you."

"Well, from the looks of everything, I would say you outdid yourself, my lovely lady." He then took a sip of his wine and sat his glass on the countertop. "Stay right here! There's something I want to give you." Then Tony anxiously walked over to the front door, opened it, and pulled in a very large painting.

"What are you doing?" asked Jade.

"You'll see, but first close your eyes," he answered.

"Are you serious?" she asked, questioning what he wanted her to do. "Yes, and you will see why."

"Okay, they're closed," she said with one hand over both eyes.

He pulled the painting all the way in and closed the door behind. "Alright, you may open them now," he said.

As soon as Jade uncovered her eyes, her mouth opened wide from disbelief. "OH, MY GOD! You didn't!" she responded in complete shock.

"Yes, I did, and it's all yours," Tony replied.

"For me? Wow, did you know that's an oil painting I've been eyeing for almost a year now? Not only is it one of the featured paintings in the gallery, but it costs nearly three grand!" She rubbed her hand across the top of the ambrosia frame. "How did you know which one I wanted?" Jade asked.

"Ahh… my lovely lady, I remember everything you say. Plus, I really wanted to do something special for you, and I know how much you like fine art. However, I did have help from a little birdie," he said.

"It was Sasha, right? I know it was her," said Jade as she tried to guess who told him.

"One never reveals his sources," said Tony smiling.

"Wait! You did say you're in some kind of home furnishing business, right?"

"Yes, I am," he answered, wondering where she was going with the question.

"So, do you attend art showings also because I've never seen you at any here in the city," she said.

"Well, let's just say I do know a little something about fine art myself."

"Really?" asked Jade, looking confused from his answer. "Oh, okay, well, I guess we have more in common than I thought."

"I guess we do," he replied with a smile and lightly kissed her hand.

"Thank you so much for the painting!" she excitedly said. Then after a pause… "I'm not even sure I should be accepting this kind of gift from you. I mean, it's so expensive and way too soon. Don't get me wrong. I'm overjoyed and honored at the same time, but—"

Before Jade could finish speaking, he put his index finger over her lips. "Shhh… I want you to have this, and it would mean a lot to me if you would keep it," said Tony, then he gently grabbed her hand.

"Okay, if you insist," she said and reached out to give him a hug.

Right before Jade moved away, Tony softly kissed her lips. She embraced it, and this time, she kissed him back. The sound of passion is all that could be heard.

"Ummm… I didn't know you could kiss like that," he said softly, letting off her lips.

Jade smiled as she gazed into his eyes. "I think we should have dinner now," she suggested, snapping out of her astonished mood.

"I was just thinking that too. Yeah, you do have a brother over here starving."

Jade looked at Tony and laughed. "Come on here, let's eat then." She grabbed him by the arm, and they walked over to the dining room area to have dinner.

"Wow… everything looks nice. You really did outdo yourself, my lovely lady that you are," he said while stroking the side of her face with his fingers. "Oh, here, let me get that for you," he said, pulling the chair out for Jade to sit on.

"Thanks. I hope you enjoy it. I thought a man of your stature would like a nice, fulfilling meal."

"Yes, you guessed right, and I'm pretty sure I will love it!"

Jade smiled. "Good, 'cause a sister gotta feed her man, right?" They both laughed. "Okay, let's say grace so we can eat."

"Yeah, let's do that," said Tony, stretching his hand across the table to hers. They both closed their eyes and bowed their heads.

It was about 10 o'clock when Jade and Tony wrapped up dinner. Jade was sitting comfortably on the loveseat, with one leg folded under her bottom, when Tony walked up to her.

"Care to dance?" he asked and reached for Jade's hand.

"Sure, I would love to dance with you," she answered then stood and positioned herself in front of him. With one arm around Jade's waist, he embraced her body while their other hands intertwined, and they slow danced to the sweet sounds of smooth jazz. "This is nice. It reminds me of our first dance on the Queen," she said, resting her head on his muscular chest.

"Yes, I remember that, and I'll remember this night too," Tony said. Then he slightly lifted her head and kissed the fullness of her lips. Jade slowly met him the rest of the way as their lips gently touched and their tongues met. They French kissed passionately for about three minutes, then things got heated, and they made their way to the couch.

"Ahhh… Umm… You are so sexy, and your lips are so soft," he expressed and worked his way around her neck.

"Umm, and you are—" Before Jade could finish speaking, passionate kisses were placed at the center of her chest, right above her cleavage. With much infatuation, Tony then worked his way along her shoulders, then he backed up to her lips again.

"I can do this all night, my love, but it's getting late, and I have a business seminar to attend in the morning." Slowly lifting himself off Jade, he straightened his clothes, drank the last bit of his wine, then looked at the time on his black, diamond designer watch.

"I understand, and it is getting late; however, I really enjoyed your company tonight," said Jade. "I'm definitely looking forward to many more," she added, gazing into Tony's eyes, "You are a very handsome man, Mr. Jacobs."

"Thank you, babe, and you're beautiful," he replied. "By the way, my love, dinner was absolutely wonderful. Yeah, I must admit there's a little Betty Crocker in you," he added with a chuckle. She chuckled also then got up from the couch to straighten her clothes and hair.

"You're fine and gorgeous as ever," he softly said as he kissed her hand.

Jade blushed and bashfully lowered her head. He grabbed her arm then pulled her closer to him. "I look forward to many more nights like this also, and to be completely honest, I don't really want to leave."

Their eyes connected again as Jade placed her hands on his shoulders and began massaging them in a slow circular motion. "A little tight, are we?" Jade asked as she continued her slow movements.

While enjoying every moment of it, Tony closed his eyes, wishing he didn't have to go so soon. "Ummm… my lady has that special touch a man needs in his life. Baby, you're making me want to sign up for the next seminar," he said and chuckled.

"Let me walk you to the door before I make you stay with me tonight," Jade replied.

Tony smiled, "That's not a bad idea, you know. Wait, did I just say that?"

"Well, we wouldn't have gone any further than we did tonight. I don't want us to move too fast," she added.

"I know that. I can tell the kind of woman you are and respect that," he replied. "Okay, I really must get going now. Remember, I have that seminar, and it's very important that I attend," said Tony. He gave Jade a goodnight kiss and hug, then she opened the front door for him.

"Be sure to call me once you get settled," she said.

"I will, and thanks again for dinner, love," he replied.

Jade smiled and began closing the door slowly. Then suddenly, she paused midway and quickly opened it back up. "Hey, thanks again for the painting!"

He smiled and continued down the hallway. She then closed and locked the door with a huge grin on her face. "Well, I should be getting myself ready for work tomorrow," Jade said and walked over to the table in a joyful mood. She immediately started clearing the remaining dishes that she and Tony used. Jade then showered and prepared for bed.

Before she could pull her gold, satin comforter over her body, a text message came through. It read: *Hello love, I know it's been a little while, but I just had to reach out to you. I hope all is well with you and the kids, and I'm looking forward to seeing you again real soon. Stay beautiful. Blaine.*

Jade sat quietly staring at her cell phone in awe. *It can't be him!* She thought, *Or could it? Blaine Thomas, the man I used to love and wanted to spend the rest of my life with, just texted after two years of being away? What could he be thinking? How does he know if I'm happily married or involved with someone else? Should I reply? No. I'm not responding. He should have contacted me way before now,* thought Jade, and she put her cell phone on the nightstand. She then said her goodnight prayer and turned off her light.

"Blaine Thomas," she mumbled as she tossed and turned, trying to get him off her mind. *I wonder how he's doing,* Jade thought and turned on the light again. Then she reached for her phone and attempted to text him back. Before she could begin typing the message, her cell phone rang. "Oh, my God. It's Tony," she said and nervously answered the call. "Hey, baby, I'm guessing you're home now."

"Yes, love, and thinking about you and the time we shared together to night. You are so beautiful to me, and your lips… ummm, I can kiss them all night long."

Jade began blushing and propped herself up on her satin pillows. "I can kiss you all night, too, with your fine self."

"Well, my lovely lady, I just wanted to hear your sexy voice before I get some shut eye. So, sweet dreams, and I will touch base with you after my meeting is over," he said and blew her a kiss through the phone.

She smiled. "Okay, sweet dreams to you, too, and I'll look to hear from you sometime tomorrow," replied Jade and blew him a kiss back.

As soon as they ended their call, Jade reopened the text from Blaine, debating whether to reply to his message or not. She figured she probably should not be texting him, but she decided to give it a try. *Hello,* she texted back then laid the phone back down on the nightstand.

"Maybe that really wasn't meant for me. Someone just had the wrong number. That's all..." Jade uttered. She then got herself comfortable, so she could get some rest. *See, it was no reply. I knew it was the wrong number, but it did say Blaine at the end.* She pondered for a moment.

Bzz... Bzz! "Another text right when I am all snuggled in. It's probably Sasha being nosy, wanting to know what happened on my date with Tony," she said, and she picked up her cell phone to read the message. It read: *Hello to you, too, and how have you been? I'm glad you responded, as I was hoping you would. I really can't wait to see you again, Jade. Please know that I miss you so much, and you have been on my mind ever since we parted. I can't say too much right now; but just know, I will be back real soon. Have to go now. Stay beautiful. Blaine.*

"So, it was him," Jade said as a tear rolled down her face. "Why now, Blaine, when I'm establishing a new relationship with a really good man who I'm happy with? Oh, Lord, what am I going to tell Tony?"

4

It was the next morning, and Jade took a jog through Central Park. "Oh, I just love Saturdays," said Jade as she fixed her earphones in her ear and stretched her legs before she began jogging.

She took off down the path, which surrounded a huge pond. Jade jogged through a crowd of people who were sightseeing, bicycling, and fishing in the park.

Ahh… This is so refreshing and much needed after that big surprise Blaine laid on me last night. I still don't know how to handle this, but I know who does! My girl, Sasha, she thought and placed her Bluetooth on her right ear.

Ring! Ring! "Hello?"

"Hey, girl! What are you doing? I need to talk to you about something." "Ahh… Do you know what time it is?"

"Yes, it's 8 o'clock on a Saturday morning," Jade answered.

"Right! So, why are you calling me this early? You know how I am about getting my beauty sleep," replied Sasha.

"Girl, people are already in the park, and that's where I am now, getting my jog in before I go to the boutique."

"Only in New York," said Sasha laughing. "Okay, what is it? Did Mr. Bling stand you up or something?"

"No, this is not about Tony. It's about Blaine."

"What?" she asked, surprised at her reply. "Okay… What about Mr. Lover Boy?"

"Sasha, quit playing. This isn't funny. He texted me last night right before I got ready to go to bed."

"Really? What did he say?" asked Sasha. "Wow, the nerve of him contacting you after so long."

"That's how I felt too," said Jade.

"Well, what did he say?" Sasha asked again. "Wait… don't tell me he wants to waltz his way back into your life like you're still single and sitting around, twiddling your thumbs, and waiting for him to come back. I don't think so!" Sasha sarcastically said.

"He didn't say much about us, but he did say he missed me and that he will be back real soon," Jade replied.

"Okay, so what are you going to do then?" asked Sasha.

"I have to tell Tony about him today when he calls me."

"Well, it's not like you have feelings for the guy anymore. Or, do you?"

"No. I don't love him like I used to, but I do still have some feelings for him, though," Jade replied.

"Right, of course you do, and from the sound of y'all's relationship, how could you not?" said Sasha. "I agree. You should tell Tony about him soon," she added.

"Thanks for listening, Sasha. I'm going to finish my jog, and I'll catch up with you later."

"No problem, girly. Oh, by the way, have you heard anything from Zoe this morning?" asked Jade.

"No, nothing yet," answered Sasha.

"Okay, good. I guess she's still working today then," said Jade. "I love that girl. She's so dedicated," Jade added.

"Hey, what about me?" asked Sasha. "Never mind. Don't even answer that." They both chuckled.

"I'll see you later, girly. Bye."

Jade drove down Madison Avenue toward the boutique. *I wonder how Jayden and Brittany are doing,* she thought, driving and searching for her lip gloss at the same time. "Found it!" Jade exclaimed and pulled out a neutral shade and put it on her lips. "Darn! There's never anywhere to park down here, and where is my valet man? He always took care of my clients and me, but now he's nowhere to be found. I guess I'll park at the hotel across the street— at least my baby will be okay there."

Jade pulled into the lot and noticed a man all suited up with the same body structure as Tony. He had walked through the lobby doors of the Upper West Hotel. *Is that who I think it is?"* she wondered. *Nah, and why would he be walking in a hotel with a beautiful woman like her? Okay, snap out of it! Maybe it wasn't him with another woman going into a nice, elegant, upscale hotel such as the Upper West. Well, I won't worry about that right now. I have Blaine to deal with; maybe it's nothing to worry about anyway.*

Jade pulled up further into the hotel parking lot, and a valet came to her window. "Hello ma'am. Can I help you?" asked a brown, curly-haired young man. He then tapped her window, trying to get her attention. She jumped.

"Oh, I didn't hear you the first time," Jade said. "Hello, and yes. Can you take care my vehicle for me?" she asked in a daze and handed him her valet key.

"Sure, ma'am. I'll take good care of it for you. Hey! By the way, aren't you the manager of the boutique across the street?"

"Why, yes, I am."

"I thought so; plus, you look like a woman of high fashion," he politely said.

Jade smiled. "Thank you. I will see you shortly, dear," she said and walked across the street.

"Hey, Zoe, what's going on around here?"

"Nothing much. We're just doing the markdowns for the clearance sale next week," she replied.

"So, how are you doing?" asked Zoe.

"Sasha told you, right?" Jade asked her.

"Yeah, she called me here this morning. That's so bizarre. What do you think he wants?" Zoe asked on her way to get hangers from the rack.

"I have no clue. Maybe just to say hi and see how the kids and I are doing," replied Jade.

"Call me foolish, but maybe he wants you back," said Zoe.

"Well, I sure don't know why he wants to see me now after all this time, and you know, I've been seeing a lot of Tony lately. Speaking of Tony, I think I saw him walking in the Upper West Hotel across the street with another lady."

"Huh?" Zoe questioned, then she looked at Jade with her mouth dropped open and her eyes wide. "You didn't… How do you know it was him, and why would he be going in a hotel with some lady?" asked Zoe.

"I asked myself the same question. I don't know," Jade replied, then she walked over to look out the window. "I'm pretty sure it was, and I'm definitely going to ask when we talk," she added.

"Hey, where is Sasha? Shouldn't she be here by now?" asked Zoe as she hung the rest of the skirts she had marked down.

"Yeah… well, you know, Sleeping Beauty has to get her sleep." They both laughed.

"She'll probably be here any minute now," said Jade as she went over to help Zoe with the skirts.

The boutique door swung open. "Hello, girlies!" Sasha said then pranced in the boutique as if the world was hers.

"Hey, Sasha!" they both said at the same time.

"What y'all up to?" asked Sasha.

"We were just talking about you," replied Zoe. Then she chuckled.

Jade laughed. "You two are so funny and always at it, in a sister kind-of-way that is," said Jade.

"Sasha knows she's my girl," replied Zoe and walked over to hug her.

"Yeah… yeah, enough already. Let's get some work done here because I have a lunch date with Mike at noon today," said Sasha.

"Hey, how's he doing these days?" asked Jade as she started looking through her client book.

"Oh, he's doing good. That promotion has really allowed us to do more, and he just bought me a new diamond bracelet," Sasha answered and held out her arm to show it off.

"Wow… that's nice," said Zoe.

"Wait. Let me get a look at that," said Jade and ran over for a close up. "Oh… Sasha, that is beautiful! I didn't know Mike had it in him."

"Whatever...."

"No, just kidding. Tell him I said that was really nice. By the way, guess what Tony bought me, and you are not going to believe it."

"What?" Zoe and Sasha said at the same time.

"Remember the painting I've been eyeing the last year? Well..." said Jade looking at them both.

"No, he didn't!" said Sasha.

"Okay, he is just too generous," said Zoe.

"Yes, he is," Jade agreed and went to check her cell phone to see if she had any missed calls. "Tony didn't call me yet, so I'm guessing he's still busy," she sadly said and placed her phone back in her purse.

"Girl, he will call soon, so don't even worry about that. The lady you saw with him probably wasn't anyone but an old college friend or something," said Zoe waving her hand.

"Huh... What? You saw Tony with some other woman?" asked Sasha, running over near Jade to see what was going on.

"Hey, I'm not going to make a big deal out it, but yes, I believe he went into the Upper West Hotel earlier with an attractive woman. She doesn't have anything on me, but still she was nice looking," said Jade then walked away from Sasha.

"Well, it better be nothing," said Sasha with one hand resting on her hip.

"That's right!" yelled Zoe.

"Aww... That's why I love you two because you'll always have my back—no matter what. Come on, let's get these clothes marked down, so missy over there can go on her lunch date."

Jade headed home after a long afternoon at the boutique. "Hello, Mr. Franklin!" she yelled and speeded past where he stood, looking all sharp in his navy-blue uniform.

"Jade, my dear. How's it going?" he asked as he always does when he sees her.

"I'm good. Thank you." Jade yelled back while rushing toward the elevator doors.

"That Ms. Taylor is something else," he muttered and smiled, shaking his head.

Jade opened the front door to her luxury apartment. "I think I'll catch up on some reading tonight after I check my email," she said and locked the door behind her. Skittles jumped with excitement while Jade kicked off her stilettos and tossed her purse onto the couch. "I had a very interesting day," Jade said while petting the top of the dog's head. "Uhmm… A bubble bath sure sounds good to me right now. Let me see what kind of scents I have left," she said and went over to look at her collection of fragrances. *Okay, 'Tropical Romance,' yeah, this will do it. Ahhh… This feels so good,* Jade thought after sitting in the tub. She rested her head back and positioned herself comfortably in the steamy, hot bubble bath.

Jade closed her eyes to reminisce about the time she spent with Tony. *Why can't I seem to get that sight of them out my mind, and why hasn't he called me yet?* Jade wondered. *It's going on 7 o'clock in the evening, and that's not like him at all. He's usually good with touching base with me. Okay, snap out of it, Jade!* She propped her leg up on the side of the tub and sank down a bit further for the bubbles to completely cover her body. Jade dosed off and took a short catnap for a few minutes before being awakened by the phone ringing. "It's Tony!" Jade was excited and quickly grabbed for her phone. "Hello, Tony," she said in a low tone.

"Hello to you, too, my lovely lady. Sorry, I'm just getting in touch with you. It's been a long day, and the seminar lasted longer than I anticipated," he explained.

"Hey, I understand you were busy," Jade replied.

"Yes, I was. Plus, I had no reception in that place anywhere," Tony added.

"Oh, well… my day wasn't too bad. I was able to go jogging through the park and went into the boutique for a few hours. Now I'm relaxing in a tub of bubbles."

"Wow… that really sounds good. Can I come join you?" Tony asked with a short chuckle.

"Sure, you can! When should I expect you?" she playfully asked.

"I'm on my way right now!" They both laughed. "I was just teasing you, my love. Enjoy this relaxation time, and if you like, we can talk when you get settled. Although I would like to be in there soaking with you, there's plenty of time for that," he said.

"You are such a gentleman," replied Jade. "That's what I love about you the most. Oh, uhmm… Tony, I have something to ask you before we get off the phone."

"Sure, what is it?"

"Where was your seminar held at today?" she asked.

"Yeah, I meant to tell you that we were going to be across from your store—"

"Boutique!" Jade jokingly yelled.

"Yes, I'm sorry. I wanted to mention it to you last night, but it kind of slipped my mind," Tony replied. "Please forgive me, love." Jade then cracked a small grin.

"Hey, if it makes you feel better, there were times I couldn't focus on what the guy was saying. You had my mind all clouded up."

She smiled. "Well, I had to park at the hotel today, and when I pulled up, I thought I saw you walking in with some tall, slim, attractive lady," said Jade.

"Oh… you must be talking about Trina, my cousin. Yeah, she's a businesswoman like yourself. We probably had just finished talking about her and her husband's business out in Chicago," Tony replied.

"I would've introduced you two, but she flew in just for the seminar. Wait. Please tell me you didn't think something else in that pretty mind of yours."

Jade smiled. "Well…. I just thought to ask, that's all."

"I understand. I'd have done the same if I had seen you with another man," he replied.

"Speaking of another man, there's something I need to tell you," said Jade. "Okay, go for it," said Tony.

"I used to date this guy named Blaine a few years ago, and he contacted me the other night."

"Go on…"

"We were really into each other. You could say we were in love, and the only reason it didn't work out was because he had to go away on business. He has some top-secret job that required him to leave the states for a couple years."

"What does this have to do with our relationship?" asked Tony.

"In his message, he said he'll be back soon, and he's looking forward to seeing me."

"Tell me… Do you still love him?"

"No, but I have to be honest with you. There was talk about us getting married, but I couldn't deal with us having a long-distance relationship, so he left, and I slowly, but surely, moved on," she replied.

"So, to answer your question, yes, there are still some feelings there; however, I don't love him like I did."

"Well, I can respect your honesty, and I love you even more for that, my lovely lady. I can see why he would want to marry you. You're an incredible woman, and your beauty is like a rose that continues to bloom. Know this: I'm here; first, as your friend, and then, your lover," he said humorously. "Nah… all jokes aside, I won't put any pressure on our relationship. You're the kind of lady I want to unfold petal-by-petal."

Jade cracked a smile. "Thank you for what you just said. It means a lot to me. Alright! Now that's out of the way, when am I going to see that handsome face of yours again?" she asked.

"Oh, I'm one step ahead of you. I was going to ask you to go away with me for the upcoming weekend," he replied. "I would've said one whole week, but I want to take it slow with you, so you'll know I'm here because I really like you."

"Are you serious? Away? Where to?" Jade asked excitedly.

"Let's just say: My private jet will be able to get us to the island in no time, but you have to bring a swimsuit, and be ready to go swimming with the fish."

"Okay, I accept your invitation. To the islands we go…" she said and prepared to get out of the tub.

"Good! It should be a lot of fun," said Tony. "We will touch base on that later in the week to confirm everything. My love, I'm really glad you said yes."

Jade smiled. "Well, I'm going to step out of my bath now, and I will send you a nice little text message to go to bed with."

"Okay, I'll look forward to it. Talk soon, love," he said before hanging up the phone.

Jade and Tony are vacationing in the Cayman Islands while Sasha and Zoe run the boutique.

"Ooh… look, girly, these are so fly," said Sasha and held a pair of blue, ripped-cut skinny jeans to her waist.

"Yeah, that's the style now. Rip-and-wear, distressed jeans," said Zoe.

"Yeah, I know. I saw Lola with a pair on last week. She had on a nice pair of peep-toe pumps with hers. You know how she does it."

"Yup, sure do," answered Zoe.

"So, what are your plans for tonight?" asked Sasha.

"I don't have any. Come to think of it, maybe you and I can hang out a bit tonight if you don't have anything else to do," Zoe replied.

"Hey, that's sounds like fun. Let's go to that Japanese steakhouse everyone raves about. You know, the one where they cook your food in front of you," said Sasha.

"Okay, that's fine. Plus, I haven't eaten a good Asian dish in a while," said Zoe and placed a blouse on the hanger.

"Mama Mia… Mama Mia!" said Sasha after she glanced out the window. "What is wrong with you?"

"Girly, nothing. Look at this fine man getting ready to walk in," she answered.

"Ummm… You weren't kiddin'! He's hot and strong and…. Hush, here he comes."

"Hello, ladies."

They both stood speechless for a moment. "Ahhh, hello. Can we help you?" asked Sasha.

"I'm looking for Jade Taylor. This is her boutique, isn't it?" the mystery man asked.

"Yes, it is," said Zoe. Then she walked over to shake his hand. "I'm Zoe. Sorry, but Jade is out of town and won't be back until the morning. Oh, by the way, that's Sasha over there. Please excuse us, but we don't see too many men of your build and good looks around here very often."

"Oh, now I understand," he said and chuckled. "Well, hello over there, Ms. Sasha. I've heard so much about you. I'm Blaine Thomas, an old friend of Jade's."

Sasha and Zoe looked at each other and then back at him. "You're Blaine? We have heard a lot about you! It's nice to finally meet the man who left our girl heartbroken," said Sasha.

"Hey, I understand your feelings and concerns for your friend. I also care for her. Plus, there's something I need to tell Jade that I've been waiting until I returned," he said.

Silence filled the boutique for a moment. "Well, I'm sure Jade will be very surprised to see you. By the way, does she know you're here in town?" asked Zoe.

"No, she doesn't, and I want it to be a surprise. So, I guess I'll have to catch up with Jade tomorrow then," he said and prepared to leave the boutique.

"Okay, we will keep our mouths sealed," said Zoe.

"Yeah, I'll try to," said Sasha. Blaine opened the door and headed out. "Hey, just make sure you don't hurt my friend," Sasha added.

"Trust me… That's not what I'm here for. I'm here because I never stopped loving Jade," he said before the door closed.

"Girl, can you believe the nerve of him? It sounds like he wants to waltz his way back into her life."

"I know…. Men, I tell ya," said Zoe then shook her head.

"But I will say one thing… he sure is fine!"

They both laughed and high-fived each other. "Yes, indeed!" Zoe agreed.

"Oh, girly, look at the time! Let's wrap it up around here, so we can go get our eat on. I'm getting hungry, and the thought of a good cuisine sounds good to my stomach," said Sasha.

"Okay, I'll start straightening while you close the register out," replied Zoe.

"That's a plan. Hey, we didn't do too bad today, and I'm going to hook myself up with a pair of those fly jeans," said Sasha as she went to finish counting the cash.

5

Jade and Tony returned home from their weekend getaway.

While lying out in the sun on her luxury, custom designed terrace lounger, Jade picked up her cell phone to place a call. "Hey, babe, it's me! I just want to tell you that that vacation was just what I needed. Thank you so much for thinking of something like that. I love a man of spontaneity. It keeps the relationship interesting."

"It was my pleasure, love. I'm looking forward to much more traveling with you.

Maybe we can do a cruise or something within a few months. I just need a little time to make the necessary arrangements," said Tony.

"A cruise would be nice, but let's recover from the trip we just came back from before we're off on another—but keep that thought." Jade giggled.

"Oh, trust me. I will," Tony replied. "So, what are you up to today other than talking with me on this pleasant summer afternoon?"

"Just lying out on my terrace, thinking if I want to go to the art gallery to see what new paintings they have."

"Really? That doesn't sound like a bad idea. I'm pretty sure they have some new pieces in their shipment. Probably was delivered not too long ago, so you can get first pick," said Tony.

"Wow! You sound like you know the gallery like the back of your hand. So, why don't you come along with me? I'm sure you will love it!" said Jade.

"Oh no… That's okay. You go on and enjoy your outing. Just let me know what you saw and liked," he said.

"Are you sure? I know you're in that line of business, but you can still visit other furniture stores too," Jade added.

"Yes, you are absolutely correct, but I'm going to pass on this offer. Just know you will be in my thoughts as you always are. Now, you go on, and we can talk later tonight."

"Okay, you have a good day as well, babe," said Jade and ended the call.

It was around 6 o'clock on Tuesday evening when Jade decided to go to the gallery. She entered through the large, fancy, brass-trimmed door and began browsing around. "Ahh… This is really nice," Jade said, admiring a beautiful modern sculpture. She decided to take notes on it.

Slowly, Jade walked a little further and saw something else that caught her eye. This was a masterpiece of art: one of the gallery's newest and most attractive oil paintings displayed. "Gorgeous!" Jade softly said and began writing in her notepad.

"Not as gorgeous as you are," said the man who stood next to her. She quickly stopped writing after hearing that deep, masculine, sexy voice that sounded so familiar. With her back still facing the painting, a kiss was placed on her cheek. She dropped her pen and pad, and then she turned around to see a tall, bald, 6'2", chocolate man with arms of steel standing with a red rose in his hand.

"Oh, my God! Blaine, is it really you?"

"Yes, it's me in the flesh," he said, picking her up in his arms and giving Jade a big hug.

"When did you get back, and how did you know I was here?" she asked excitedly.

"Yesterday," he answered. "I went to your boutique, but your girls said you were out of town and would be back today. Plus, I remembered the days you liked to check the gallery for new artwork. So, I took my chances on coming here, only to find the most beautiful piece of art in this place."

Jade smiled as a tear rolled down her face. Blaine took his hand and wiped the tear away then gave her the rose. "Baby, you don't know how much I missed you! All I thought about everyday was you and the kids while I was away. It was really hard leaving you like that—Not hearing your voice for as long as I did was even harder for me," said Blaine. "I used to pick up the phone to call you and then put it down because I didn't want to complicate things. Also, it wouldn't have been fair to either one of us. I felt it was better to leave you alone and let you live your life happily," Blaine explained.

Jade remained speechless as she absorbed every word he said. "We were so happy together but I had to move on, and it wasn't easy because—" There was a slight pause. "— I was in love with you," she replied.

Blaine pulled her closer. "When you said you've moved on, are you speaking of being involved with someone else?" Blaine asked curiously. Before she could open her mouth, he said, "Baby, remember the night we parted ways? Well, I was going to ask you something, but I couldn't because the timing wasn't right. So, before you answer that question, let me ask you one thing," Blaine said.

She looked at him with confusion on her face as he got down on bended knee. "Jade, baby, I need you to know that I love you with all my heart, soul, and might, and I always have. Although there was some distance between us, I always knew you were the one for me," he said and took her right hand. She covered her mouth with the other and began to shiver as tears started to flow.

"Baby, I'm down on bended knee because I can't seem to be without thee… You complete me in every way, and so, humbly, I take this God-given day to say, 'I need you.' So, Jade, the love of my life, will you marry me?" he asked holding a stunning, three carat, platinum diamond ring up in one hand.

With her eyes all watered, she tried to answer, but couldn't get the words together, so she ran out of the gallery, crying.

"Jade!" He yelled for her to stop, but she continued running. Blaine then ran out the door after her but couldn't see through the rain as it began to pour down harder. "Jade!" he yelled again with tears forming in his eyes, walking toward the parked cars.

Blaine approached his black, shiny truck, and he noticed a lady sitting in an SUV next to it. It was Jade - sitting there, laying across the steering wheel and crying. Not aware of his presence, she took out her cell phone to call Sasha, but the disturbance of soft tapping on the window caught her attention.

"Jade, is that you?" Blaine asked while trying to see through the rain and light fog. After recognizing the voice, she cracked her window just enough to make sure it was who she thought it was.

"Yes, it's me," Jade softly said and wiped her eyes with her hands to see more clearly. "Please get in," she told him. He quickly ran around to the other side and hopped in her SUV. Then soaking wet, Blaine leaned over, grabbed her face, and passionately kissed Jade on the lips, but she quickly pulled back.

"I can't do this! There's someone else now. We met a couple of months ago, and things have been really good ever since," Jade said.

"So, that explains why you ran away from me," he replied and slightly lowered his head. "Do you love him? How well do you know this guy?" asked Blaine as the questions continued to come at her.

"Yes, I have developed strong feelings, and I believe I'm falling in love with him," she answered. "I was even thinking about him meeting the kids when they return."

Silence filled the air for a moment. "Baby, we were together for nearly three years, and I know me having to leave hurt you. Hey, it hurt me, too, but I'm back now," he said and softly stroked her cheek.

Jade looked in his direction. "Listen, don't get me wrong. I understand duty called, but you were gone for some time," she said and gently placed her hand on his chest.

"Yes, and I didn't even expect to come back this soon, but it all worked out where I wasn't needed anymore," Blaine replied. "Man, I guess my big plans for us are gone down the drain now."

"What plans?" asked Jade, turning her body completely around to face him.

"You know all the properties I own? Well, they were for us to own together. I had you in mind when I bought a villa in Casa DeLeon on an island in the Bahamas. Even though you've decided to move on, I still want you to have this," he said and handed her an envelope with her name on it.

Jade looked confused. "I don't understand," she replied then read the paper inside. It listed her as the owner of a property with all the details. It was a 2-story, 8,435 square foot, ocean view villa with 2 VIP bedrooms, a steam shower, jacuzzi, a huge atrium, an infinity pool, wet bar, and so on. "No way. I can't accept this from you," she said and shoved it back at him. "Blaine, I can't do this anymore. I have someone else in my life now."

"Yes, you told me, but I bet he doesn't love you like I do, nor can he take care of you like I can." Before he could finish his sentence, she broke out in tears. He grabbed Jade by the arm and pulled her close, and her head rested on his muscular chest. "I'm sorry, baby. This is really hard for me, and, of course, I don't want to let you go," Blaine said then wiped the tears from her face and softly kissed her forehead. "Okay, how about this? Let's go to my hotel room and spend some more time together, and I'll think about letting you go."

Jade looked up and saw him smiling. "You know what..." she paused for a moment, "Never mind!" Then after playfully hitting his arm, Jade shook her head. "Well, now, I am trying to wait until I get married to have sexual intercourse. Again, that is!" she exclaimed.

"Okay, I understand. I can respect that. I see we can't go back to when we both wanted it, which you have to admit, were some passion-filled nights," replied Blaine. "Times I will never forget," he added and handed her back the envelope.

With her heart pounding from the memories, she hesitantly took it from him.

"Hey, this is for you and the kids! Please accept it! Just remember that I love you and always will, no matter what, and I'm always gonna be here for you."

"Blaine, I know that, but I'm sorry I can't take this," Jade said and quickly handed the envelope back to him. "Besides, what would Tony think if I accepted something like this from you?"

"What do I care what he thinks?" Blaine took the envelope from her hand. Jade looked surprised at his reply and slowly lowered her head. Blaine noticed the sad look on her face. Then he used his hand and gently lifted her head back up. "Just be happy and let me know if you ever have any problems out of that guy."

He softly stroked the side of her face with his fingers, then Jade closed her eyes and embraced his touch. Quickly, she snapped out of it. "Hey, maybe you can meet him someday," she said, "or not," Jade quickly added.

"Nah… I don't know about that," he said, trying to keep his spirits lifted even though his heart was broken. Blaine opened the car door and stepped out. "It was real nice seeing your lovely face again, Jade. Stay beautiful," he said and pushed his remote to unlock the doors to his truck. "By the way, what's the guy's name?" asked Blaine.

"Tony. Tony Jacobs," she answered. He got quiet for a moment.

"Hey!" Jade yelled, disrupting his sudden silence and deep thought. "It was nice seeing you again too," she said. After she took one last look at his fine, chocolate body, she prepared to drive off.

"Wait!" Blaine yelled out. Jade quickly looked up and rolled her window down. "That name sounds very familiar to me."

"Who are you talking about?" asked Jade, staring at him in confusion. "Tony Jacobs!" he replied.

"Yeah, what about him?"

"Isn't he the owner of the art gallery we just left? Even though I wish you had visited mine instead," said Blaine with a serious face. "You know, I own one also. Plus, remember, it's where I first said I love you?"

"Yes, I remember, but no, he does not," Jade replied. "Why would you think that? He works with Mike at that big marketing firm over on Wall Street," she replied confidently. "Oh, but wait! He did say he has a side business in 'home furnishing', but it was just something small, I think," Jade said then paused in thought.

"Well, that's not small at all because I believe there's one with the same name in Washington, DC, also," Blaine said.

"Yes, I heard it's really nice too. They're always sending me invites to their art shows, but I haven't made it to DC yet," Jade replied.

"Okay, baby, I just thought it was a little ironic that you were dating him and didn't mention who he was," Blaine said.

"I didn't know his name was important to you. Although, I'm still not sure if we're talking about the same person. Plus, I'm pretty sure he would have mentioned something like that to me by now," Jade said.

"Yeah, I guess you're right. Why wouldn't he tell you that he's the owner of the art gallery his lady goes to on a regular basis? Man, the sound of that…. 'His lady'. Okay, I better get going now and let you be on your way too," Blaine said sadly and started his truck.

"Yes, it's getting late," replied Jade after looking at the time and then up at his saddened face. "Hey, I'm still around and still your friend," she said, hoping it would make everything all right.

"Yup. Same here," he replied with a fake grin, trying not to show his real feelings. She grinned slightly and drove away.

It was 6:30 a.m. when Jade's alarm clock went off on a hot, sunny Thursday morning. "Ahhh… that felt good," she said after yawning and stretching before getting out of bed. "Thank You, Lord, for allowing me to see another one of Your beautiful days," Jade said and glanced out her huge bay window. She went into the bathroom and lightly splashed warm water on her face to help her wake up.

"Now I need to check my email and get some clothes on because I have a meeting with that top designer today," Jade said then rushed to open her laptop to log in. "What? Twenty-five new emails?" she yelled. "I need to check my inbox more often or hire someone to do that for me," she said laughing at herself and began to read them one-by-one, starting with the most important.

After scrolling through her messages, she came across one from her brother. It read: *Hey Sis, I just wanted to let you know your niece, Tina, has turned into a fashion diva. She's driving her mom and me bonkers out here! Thanks a lot, Sis, for your big influence. Now, you've created a fashion monster. It's all about shoes, shoes, shoes with her. I hope you and the kids are well, and I'm looking forward to you visiting. Love ya, Zack.*

Jade smiled. "That's my girl!" she said with excitement. She replied with her plans for opening a new shoe boutique in California and how she would love to have Tina manage it someday. Jade also included that she and the kids were doing fine and that she had a new man in her life now.

After reading all of her messages, Jade leaned back in her chair and reflected on when Blaine asked if Tony owned an art gallery in Manhattan. "Now I'm wondering if it's true, and why would he hold back that kind of information from me?" she questioned. So, she decided to arrange for them to meet at Ocean Seas for dinner.

Jade immediately looked in the closet for something really classy to wear. She pulled out a burgundy, short-sleeved, v-neck, wrap dress and laid it on the bed. Then she picked out a pair of beige, pointy-toe, patent leather heels to go with it. "This should do it," Jade said and then got herself ready for work.

The boutique door swung open. "What's going on, ladies?" Jade said, removing her brown designer shades from her eyes as she spoke to Sasha and Zoe.

They both looked up from working to greet her. "Hey, girly, what's new?" asked Sasha with her New York-Puerto Rican accent.

Jade sighed. "Well, where do I begin?" she questioned and laid her purse on the counter next to the cash register. "Okay, here it goes! Blaine proposed to me last night, and I said no."

"Huh?" Zoe looked at her in disbelief.

"What, girly? He asked you to marry him?" asked Sasha. "Wow, you go from not having a man to having dinners on yachts, helicopter rides, and getting proposed to by one of the finest men I've seen in a long time."

Zoe and Jade laughed. "It's not funny because it was really emotional for the both of us," Jade explained as she stopped laughing.

"So, what romantic proposal technique did he use because I know he did something out of the norm," asked Zoe with her hand on her hip.

Jade calmly answered, "Yes, I must admit it was pretty nice—the way he showed up at the gallery unexpected and presented me with a rose."

"A rose! No ring?" Sasha asked, sounding a little upset. Zoe lightly tapped her arm then giggled at her reaction.

"Wait.… Ladies. He did present a ring to me, and it was so beautiful from what I remember."

"Okay, girly, you're losing me here. This is too much!" Sasha said, looking at Jade with a puzzled facial expression.

"Y'all, I was speechless, and I ran out of the gallery in tears," replied Jade.

"You ran? Like, ran as if someone was chasing you type-of-running?" Zoe asked in a joking way.

"Hey, that's not funny. But, yes, I did kind of," she answered.

Sasha and Zoe looked at each other then back at Jade. "I'm sorry, you're right. It's not funny at all. I was just kidding with you."

"Yeah, girly. Me too. I'm so sorry to hear that, and it must have been pretty hard seeing him again," said Sasha.

"Of course, it was, but I'm wondering how I'm going to tell Tony that I saw him," said Jade.

"So, you've never mentioned that relationship since the two of you've been dating?" asked Zoe.

"Ahh... No, and why should she?" answered Sasha, jumping in the conversation.

Jade just remained silent while the two of them continued talking. She quietly went to the back of the boutique to get some extra hangers for the new clothing line they were getting in. Zoe noticed that Jade walked off without saying anything and got concerned.

"See, look what you did, Sasha! You made her leave!"

"Who?"

"Jade, silly!"

Overhearing the fuss, Jade asked, "Are you two done now?" She walked back out to the front with both hands full of gold hangers.

"Yes, we are, and let us help you with those," said Sasha, grabbing a few from her hands. Zoe went to help also, then they placed them on the rod near the wall.

"This will be fine until the clothes come in, and I get back from my meeting with that new designer we'll be working with soon. Oh, and you'll have to see his shoe line," Jade quickly added. "Oh my, God, they are fierce!"

"Yes, girly, I've heard, and we will be the first boutique to carry them," replied Sasha.

"You got that right." Jade raised her hand to give them both high-fives. "Okay, ladies, I'm going to head out of here now, so I won't be late. We're meeting at a studio in Long Island in about an hour from now; therefore, I need to be going. The designer wanted me to come to his house, but I thought it would be better to go out this time," said Jade while scrambling for her keys. "Oh, yeah, I'm also meeting Tony for dinner this evening at Ocean Seas."

"So, you're telling him over dinner, huh?" said Zoe. "Nice," she said and smiled at Jade.

"Yeah, girly, you'll have people all around you in case he gets upset." Sasha laughed.

"I don't know what to say about y'all sometimes," Jade said and headed toward the door.

"Don't pay her any mind," said Zoe then giggled at what Sasha said.

"Okay, ladies, I will call you later, and please make sure you send out evites to our clients for the private sale and semi-fall showing. Ta-ta!" She said and put her shades on and hurried out the door.

After meeting with the new designer, Jade left to meet Tony. About fifteen minutes from her destination, her phone rang. Reaching for her purse while trying to drive, too, Jade looked at the caller ID and saw that it was Tony.

"Hey, love, I'm on my way," she said, assuming that was why he called. "No, that's not why I'm calling you," Tony replied.

"Is everything alright?"

"Yes, my lovely lady. Calm down. There's just been a change of plans. That's all," he said.

She came to a red traffic light, which allowed her to give him her full attention. "Oh, you have something else that came up?" Jade asked curiously, wanting to know what it could be.

"Yes, I want you to come out to my house this time!" he excitedly answered, hoping she'd agree.

"Oh, I see." Jade got silent for a second. "Your house? Today?" she repeated, making sure she heard him correctly.

"I know it's short notice, but I'm hoping it's alright with you," he replied. After noticing her strange reaction, he got a bit curious. "Hey, you're sounding a little distant. Is everything okay with you?" Tony asked.

"Uhmmm... so, do you need me to bring anything?" Jade asked, avoiding the question about her being okay.

"No, just your lovely self," Tony answered, being completely thrown off by her comeback; however, Jade managed to crack a small grin.

Honk! Honk! Cars began to blare their horns in the background behind her. "Oh, dear," she then said after a glance in her rearview mirror. Jade quickly drove off after being blown at to move. "Hun, text me your address, and I'll be on my way there," she said to him.

"Will do, and I can't wait to see that beautiful face of yours again." Jade tried to smile but could not because she was rather nervous about what Tony was going to say after telling him about Blaine. "Oh, well, so much for having people around when I do tell him, " she said and giggled.

Jade put her phone away but kept the Bluetooth on her ear. "Oh, yeah... Let me hurry and cancel our reservations at Ocean Seas."

Shortly after Jade received the address from Tony, she pulled up to a large, white gate with a security entrance system. *There must be some mistake,* she thought. Then she looked up at the huge, gorgeous house in front of her.

"Hello!" she yelled into the little box outside to the gate. "Is anyone home?" No one answered. "Hello? Is Tony here?" Jade asked again, still stunned by what she saw around her.

"Hey, love, you made it! One minute," Tony answered, then the gates opened up. Jade drove in very cautiously, not understanding how he lived in such a big house all by himself. After she pulled up and parked her SUV in the circular driveway, Tony hurriedly ran out to greet her with a big hug and kiss.

"Hey, glad you made it! Was it hard to find?" he asked.

"No, I found this mansion quite well, but I'm not understanding something here."

Before she could continue, he interrupted, "I know what you must be thinking."

"No, you don't," Jade said, noticing three luxury vehicles. "Are you doing something illegal? Because if so, I don't want anything else to do with you," she said directly.

He laughed then grabbed her arm to pull her close to him. "No, I'm not," Tony said, and then he softly kissed her lips.

"But you and Mike work together at a firm. He has a nice house, too, but nothing like this. Your little side job must really be helping a whole lot," she added.

"Yes, about that...... but first, let me show you around," he said, rubbing his head nervously.

Jade hesitantly walked with him into a beautiful foyer. "Tony, this is nice, and I love the cathedral ceilings, and—Oh, my God, your chandeliers are very lovely too. Who helped you decorate?" she asked.

But before he could answer, she saw some of the most beautiful art paintings on his walls. "Wow, it's like a gallery in here....so pleasing to the eye," Jade expressed. "Where did you get this piece?" Jade asked after she spotted a particular sculpture she'd seen before.

"Well... I bought it," he answered.

"Really? How? I was at the auction where it was bid on, and it sold for nearly $5,000," she replied. "Some older guy who was sitting somewhere in back of me won that bid," Jade explained.

"I know! It was Mr. Dixon, the one you met on the Queen," said Tony.

"You're kidding me, right?" she asked quickly and turned her head in his direction. While still in awe at everything she saw, Jade decided to walk over to take a seat on his very expensive, Italian, gray leather couch.

"Jade, there's something I want to share with you, which is why I asked you to come out here today. Plus, so I can show you where I live and to tell you the art gallery you've been going to, well….along with another in Paris, a small one in California, and one in Washington, DC, I'm the owner of them. I also own a little real estate in Florida," he explained while holding both her hands. "So, you see, that's how I can afford all this."

Jade looked surprised. "Why didn't you tell me this when we first met or at my house?" she asked emotionally.

"I'm the type of man who wants a woman to love me for me—not for what I own. I feel I've found that in you along with all the other wonderful attributes you possess. I believe I love you," Tony explained.

Jade sighed. "Wow I don't know where to begin." She stood up and nervously paced the floor. "Well, I have something to tell you too. Wait. You said you love me?!"

"Yes, I did, and I truly do feel that," he said and looked over at her beautiful, brown eyes. "I first felt it when we were dancing at your place that night. Jade, my love, I have been so happy over the last few months and needed to tell you that."

"Aww… that's so sweet, and thanks for sharing that with me," she replied. Her eyes began to water. Tony then placed a kiss on her cheek, and Jade nervously paced the floor again. "Okay, well, where do I begin?"

"Just say it, babe. I'm a big boy. I can handle it," Tony said curiously, wanting to know what was on Jade's mind.

"Alright, here it goes! I, too, have developed strong feelings for you, Tony, and I've been happy the last few months as well—happier than I've been in a while as far as a relationship goes; however, a couple of years ago, I was deeply in love with a man who I felt chose his work over me. He decided to go away on some big assignment, which left me heartbroken. It took some time to get through it, but I did after a while."

"Go on…, " he said.

"Mind you, we dated for a couple of years, and I was hoping he would've popped the question, but he didn't," she explained.

"Hey, I understand, and it's okay. He's gone now, and you've moved on with your life."

"Yes, but that's not it," she said and sat back down next to him. Tony looked at her in confusion. "He's back in town now."

"Who?" he asked.

"Blaine!" said Jade.

"Oh, and how do you feel about that?"

"Well… we saw each other at the art gallery. Well, your art gallery, that is," Jade chuckled. *Lord, help me!* She then prayed silently while trying to get it all out. "Blaine proposed to me at the gallery the same night, but I ran out in tears because I couldn't answer him that very moment."

"Wow, I see…," said Tony and scratched the top of his head. "So, what are you going to do about this situation?"

"I eventually told Blaine that I'm seeing someone else, and I can't accept his proposal."

"How did he take that?" Tony asked.

"Better than I thought, but he's definitely disappointed. Blaine is a wonderful guy, and I know he cares a lot about me and my kids."

"Yes, speaking of your kids, I sure look forward to meeting them someday. They sound like great children."

"Thank you, and yes, they are," she replied.

"So, this Blaine guy wants my lady back...huh? Well, I'm sorry, but she's with Tony now."

Jade smiled and gently placed a kiss on his cheek. "You're so silly!" she said.

"Hey, I got a smile out of you, didn't I?"

"Oh, I did tell him that I'm still his friend, and maybe y'all can meet one another someday."

"I don't know about all that," said Tony. "So, is that all because I would like to eat now," he said jokingly, trying to lighten the mood.

Wait. Did she say, his friend? Tony paused and thought for a moment. *Nah…* he shook his head side to side.

"Yes, that is all," answered Jade unaware of his reaction. "By the way, something sure smells good."

"Yeah, your man knows how to throw down on the grill too."

"My man, huh?" she playfully repeated.

"Come on, let's head out to the back patio," Tony said and pulled Jade outside the sliding glass doors.

"Oh, yeah, there is one other thing I meant to mention. He gave me a gift that he insisted on me having," said Jade.

"What's that, my love?"

"A piece of property for the kids and I," Jade answered, trying to be modest. "Oh, really?" Tony replied, stopping right in his tracks and turning to face Jade. "Ahh... where at?"

"On an island in the Bahamas."

Tony took a deep breath. Jade quickly added, "Not to worry though. I gave it back to him." She gently fumbled with the collar on his polo shirt.

"Hmm… the dude tried to give my lady some real estate," he mumbled under his breath. "Well, I'm glad you gave it back. Now come on; let's eat," he said and went over to the grill.

"Okay, let's eat then," she said and followed right behind him. "Thank You, Lord," Jade whispered before she walked out on the patio. "Tony, this is one spacious place you have here."

"Yeah, it can get a little lonesome at times, but having the Dixons around sure does help."

"So they live here, too, I take it?"

"Well, I wouldn't say that because they do have a home of their own in the Hamptons."

"Oh, near the water. That's nice," she said.

"My guess is, when they want to get away from me or do the grown folks thing, they go home." He laughed. Jade laughed with him.

"But I'm hoping to share all this with a special lady someday. Hey, maybe a little Tony, Jr. running around the place too."

"Yeah, I hear you," she said hesitantly after he mentioned wanting kids. Jade got silent for a moment and thought about what he had just said.

"Is everything okay, love? I see you got all quiet on me all of a sudden."

"Yes, I'm fine," she answered then playfully pushed him out the way. "Is that a basketball court I see over there?"

"Yes, and why do you seem so surprised?" asked Tony. "Like I don't know anything about balling?"

Jade laughed. "Aww… baby, I'm sorry but you just don't seem like the type to have a court at his house, that's all. A golf course, yes, but a basketball court?" she teased.

"Well, if you must know, I play, and I'm darn good too. The guys come over once a month, and we get busy out there. Plus, I played on my high school team."

Jade laughed again. "Really? You can play? I can't wait to see that!"

"Speaking of games, I have two court side tickets to the next home game, and I would love for you to join me," said Tony.

"Sure, that sounds like fun!" Jade replied. "Hey, by the way, my son plays basketball for his school."

"That's cool! Maybe we can play some one-on-one someday."

"He's good too!" Jade exclaimed.

Jade and Tony finished dinner on the patio then went back inside. "That was good, baby. I didn't know you could grill like that."

"Yeah, well… that's just one of my hidden talents," he said jokingly. "Oh, so there's more to Mr. Jacobs, I take it?"

"Of course, there is, and hopefully, you will get to see all of me," Tony replied. "Hey, I give a good foot and body massage too." She smiled. "How about I show you? Put your legs up here, so I can massage those cute feet of yours, and you can feel my skills." Jade did just what the doctor ordered and propped her legs on the couch directly in from him. Tony slowly grabbed one of her feet. He began massaging at the balls and then around her toes. Tony placed a soft kiss on her big toe. Then he worked his way up her calves with his strong, masculine grip.

"Umm… Ahh!" She moaned, enjoying every second of it.

"Can I get your shoulders for you also?" he asked.

"Sure, I would like that." Jade felt relaxed. Tony then placed his hands on her shoulders and applied pressure in the tensest spots. Caught up in moment, Jade began to doze.

"How does it feel?" Tony asked.

"Good, really good," she answered. "This is so relaxing, babe, and it's been a while since I've had one of these. Normally the girls and I would treat ourselves to a full body massage and facial."

"Well, I'm glad to assist in this department. Please let me know if there's more areas where I can provide my services." They both chuckled.

"Wow, I wasn't expecting to be pampered like this. I'm glad I came, and we were able to talk and express our feelings too," she said as she ran her hand over his dark, wavy hair.

"Yeah, me too. I've been wanting to invite you over, but I was waiting on the perfect time, and what better time than now?" Jade bashfully lowed her head as she got silent while Tony slowly moved from the back of her to the front and looked Jade in the eyes. "Stay with me tonight. I don't want you to go," he said.

"Well, I don't know about that," she hesitated.

"My love, I just want your company to remain tonight, and I promise I won't try anything. Hey, I know how ladies like to be held and cuddled, so let me give you that tonight. We can sleep right here on the couch or make a mat on the carpet," he suggested.

Jade pleasantly smiled. "Yes, I would love to stay here with you." She reached over to hug him.

Tony smiled and hugged her back. "Good, let me get us some blankets, and we can lay over by the fireplace."

He excitedly ran up his semi-spiral staircase to grab some blankets and a couple of pillows while she stayed, admiring his home and its beautiful decors. "Oh, yeah, don't forget the pillows!" Jade yelled.

"I didn't," he yelled back and came strolling down the stairs with both hands full.

She laughed. "I can hardly see your face! Here, let me help you," Jade said and reached for the blankets. "I hope right here is fine."

"Thanks, babe. I sure needed a helping hand," he said then put the blankets down on the carpet.

"Yeah, I saw that you did and thought, 'Let me help this fine man, struggling down the stairs.' "

Tony smiled. "Oh, you got jokes, huh?"

"Okay, how about we lay right here?" Jade asked.

"It's perfect since I wanted us to be in front of the fireplace. It's romantic, and I can tell you're the kind of woman who likes to be romanced. I'm here to give it to you and so much more if you will allow me," he said softly.

"Aww, Tony, see what you've done," she said getting teary-eyed.

"I'm sorry, but it's just how I feel about you. I want to help make you happy and give you the very things a woman like you desires," he explained.

"Well, just remember, I've been hurt by men before, and I don't want to be hurt again," Jade said and wiped her tears. "My heart is not to be trampled on, and when I love, I do so wholeheartedly."

"Good, because that makes two of us. Now relax and let me finish loving you," Tony said and kissed one of her hands.

Jade smiled then leaned forward and kissed his lips. "Thank you," she said then got herself comfortably down on the blanket, and Tony did the same.

"Wait! I forgot something." He quickly jumped up and went in the kitchen and came back with a bowl of strawberries and a small fondue pot.

"No, you didn't," she said when Tony walked back and placed them in front of her. "This is my favorite! How did you know?"

"Well, let's just say a little birdie told me," he answered and winked his eye at her. Sitting down next to Jade, he took a strawberry with his fingers, dipped it in the warm chocolate, and placed it in her mouth.

"Umm… this is good!" she said with the strawberry in her mouth. Tony then licked the remains off his fingertips. Jade got a strawberry and fed it to him, and she, too, licked the remaining chocolate off her fingers.

"Are you enjoying yourself so far?"

"Yes, I am, and thank you for all of this," Jade answered softly. She decided to lie down and closed her eyes to relax. "Now this is what you call cozy and romantic," Jade said. She snuggled under his arm, and he immediately embraced her.

"Umm, this feels so nice, lying here in front of the fireplace with such a beautiful woman next to me. Even though it's not burning, just the view of it and us nestled here together seem so perfect." Tony rubbed his hand through the curls in Jade's hair.

"Yes, this is beautiful, and it's been a long time since I was held like this," said Jade.

"Same here… well, it's been a little while since I've embraced a woman in my arms like this."

Silence filled the air as they both got quiet. Jade quickly placed her hand over her mouth and yawned. "Wow, excuse me. I must be getting tired," she said and closed her eyes.

"Yeah, it is kinda late," he replied, making sure the blanket covered them both. "Sweet dreams, my love." Tony softly spoke in her ear and kissed the side of her neck. *Hmmm, no response. I guess she's really tired,* he thought as he smiled and moved closer to Jade. He closed his eyes and fell off to sleep. The two peacefully lay there, snuggled next to one another.

The next morning, Tony made Jade breakfast. Jade is awakened by the smell of something cooking, so she curiously called out to Tony.

"One second!" he yelled back.

"Okay, love." She sat up and began stretching while waiting for him to come.

Walking out of the kitchen shirtless, Tony presented her with a tray of food. A small glass vase sat on top along with a pink rose inside. "Good morning, baby."

"Oh my, this is nice! You prepared all this yourself?"

"Of course, and I make the best eggs in town. I can't wait for you to try them," Tony said anxiously.

Jade smiled, then took a napkin, placed it in her lap, and said a short grace. She first decided to sip her orange juice, then took her fork, and tried the eggs. "Mmm… these are good, and that bacon looks delicious as well."

Jade happened to notice his six-pack and complimented him. "Hey, how often do you work out? With a body like that, it must be every day."

Tony looked down then placed his hands over his abs and replied, "As often as I can. With my heavy schedule, I try to get it in at least three to four days a week."

"I see," Jade said and took a bite of her bacon.

"Hold on, there, you look good yourself! I was checking out those hips and that—Never mind," he said then shook his head and chuckled.

Jade playfully hit his arm and shook her head. "Hmm, I don't know, getting spoiled with breakfast-in-bed and all." They both smiled. "I may need to work out a little more often than I have been. I'm usually good with going to my classes on a regular, but I've gotten swamped with work lately. I still try to do my daily jog in the park, which I actually love," Jade said.

"Oh, that's good. Maybe I can jog with you someday," Tony replied. "So, my sweet lady, what's on the agenda for today?"

"Well, I'm not sure, other than stop by the boutique to check on things."

"Look at you, a hard-working, dedicated businesswoman. I like it, but don't over-do it, babe. You know you have Sasha and Zoe making certain everything is going well. I'm pretty sure they have it all under control."

"Yes, baby, you're right, but I want to stop in just for a couple of hours since we are having one of our top Italian designers fly in with a new line he's promoting," Jade explained.

"Oh, okay, I see why you want to stop through now!" Tony yelled from upstairs.

"Hey, you know we can skip out of all that, and you can come up here with me. I'll give you the royal treatment after a nice swim in the pool. Then we can jump into the jacuzzi for a little while, and then move to the bedroom for some good ole relaxation. It'll be like our own little retreat. What do you say?"

"Baby, that all sounds great, and, of course, I would love to spend the day with you, but I really have to go in today," answered Jade with a look of regret on her face. *Oh, how I would rather stay with this fine man,* she thought and began reminiscing about the lovely night they shared.

"Again, I understand, my love, but I had to extend the invitation to you. Hey, it all sounded good to me, too, and I definitely look forward to spending more quality time with you," Tony added.

Jade smiled and then prepared herself to leave. "Thank you, Tony, for everything. I truly enjoyed myself with you, and I, too, look forward to spending more time with you as well. Hey, who knows? Maybe sooner than we think." Jade winked.

Tony smiled then walked Jade to her SUV. "Well, I guess this is goodbye for now, but just know I'll be thinking about you and your beautiful smile."

"Babe, how about we take a quick selfie? That way, we'll have a picture to look at when we miss one another," Jade suggested.

"Okay, let's do it!"

After taking the selfie, Jade took Tony by the hand, then she leaned in and kissed his lips. "We'll talk soon," she said and proceeded to get in her vehicle, but Tony stopped her.

"I look forward to the day we can become one. I believe that's what they call it," he told her. "Right?" Jade smiled. Tony gently grabbed her face and slowly moved in closer. They stood French kissing for about two minutes. They both became deeply engaged in the kiss until Jade slowly pulled away.

"Mmmm, that was nice. I'll definitely be thinking on that kiss all the way to the boutique," she added.

"Good, that's where I want to be…. on your mind because you'll certainly be on mine," said Tony. He closed the car door for Jade. She waved bye before she pulled off and Tony stood there, waving back. "I want her to be my wife one day," he said. Then he joyfully walked into the house.

Jade arrived at the boutique after spending a long, beautiful night with Tony. "¡Hola, chicas!" Jade said as she pushed open the glass doors of the boutique.

Zoe and Sasha both looked up in amazement of the joyful greeting they just received. "¿Hola?" Zoe quietly repeated then looked at Sasha.

"I know, right?" Sasha whispered back. "What's up with that?"

"I don't know, but I sure want to find out!" Zoe anxiously replied, and they both quickly walked over to Jade, almost knocking her down.

"Spill it!" Sasha yelled.

"Yeah, spill it! Tell us what this big smile is all about," Zoe added.

"Come on, girly. This '¡Hola, chicas!' is what got me," Sasha said with her hand on her hip and in that Spanish accent of hers. Jade just smiled and gracefully put her stuff away. She playfully acted as if she didn't even hear them.

"Okay, she must have gotten some," said Sasha.

"Yep, and it must have been good, too," Zoe added, nodding her head in agreement.

"Nope," Jade replied calmly then turned her nose up to the air. "We did not have sex."

"You didn't?" questioned Zoe.

"Oh, that's right! She went to visit Tony yesterday," Sasha blurted out.

"Yes, I did, and we had a beautiful night together. He's just the kind of man I was hoping to find one day," Jade replied with a grin on her face. "Tony is a true gentleman. He treated me with the utmost respect all night, and it got even better than that. He woke me up to breakfast-in-bed with a 3D view of that muscular chest of his. Ladies, can I keep it real? It was up close and in person, and hear me when I say, I had to restrain myself, and it wasn't easy," Jade continued, shaking her head. "Nevertheless, I know me trying to wait and us not moving too fast— well, it'll be worth it," she jokingly added with a smile.

"Wow, sounds like you really enjoyed yourself," said Sasha.

"Yes, and I also learned a lot about him too. That man is really established financially, and when I say established, that's exactly what I mean."

"Just say the man has money!" Sasha replied, teasing Jade.

"Well, we know that," Zoe chuckled.

"Why, of course. Girly, look at how he spoils you: taking you on dinner dates in jets and stuff. Who does that?" Sasha questioned. They all laughed at her New York Latina accent.

"Girl, you are too funny," said Jade and walked away from both of them.

"So obviously, you found his house okay," said Zoe as she went back to finish hanging up the new blouses they had gotten in.

"Yes, I did! Tony has the most gorgeous home. It has a white, security fence around it and sits on acres of land," Jade explained.

"Huh," replied Zoe, then she looked up with a confused facial expression.

Jade walked off while Sasha followed behind her. "Just how big is this house of his, which has to be secured like that?" Sasha asked.

"Better yet—I thought he was the one working with Mike," said Zoe.

"Right! Because my Mike has a nice house, but you sound as if Tony lives in some kind of mansion or something," Sasha added.

"Mansion is just the right word to use," Jade answered.

"What? How can he afford a big house like that doing what he does?" asked Zoe while looking very puzzled.

"I know, I know. It blew me away too. When I drove up, I thought it was the wrong address for a moment, but after looking at the text Tony sent, it was the right one! Then I saw a couple of nice vehicles lined up in the driveway, along with his fine self standing in front of them. Ladies, I was thinking to myself, *he must be selling something costly*," said Jade.

"Ah, yeah…. I would have thought the same thing," Sasha replied as she continued to put up the new sale signs.

"Well, they do earn really good money working on Wall Street, you know, especially being at one of the top marketing companies in New York," Jade added.

"Okay, but not enough to be buying mansions and flying around in jets," Sasha replied.

"You have a point there," Zoe said.

Jade got quiet then walked over to the counter and grabbed the appointment book. "He doesn't sell anything wrong, you all, but he does do something on the side," Jade explained.

"Oh, really? Yeah, that's right! You noticed that expensive ring he was wearing when the two of you met," said Sasha, thinking back to the night of their dinner. "Now, it's all coming back to me. I remember you interrogating him at the dinner table."

"Oh, I wasn't that bad," Jade replied in defense of herself.

"Oh, yes, you were!" They all laughed.

"Okay, maybe just a little."

"What am I missing here?" asked Zoe in that confused look she always has when she doesn't know what's going on.

"However, ladies, Tony did tell me he was in the home furnishing business," Jade answered.

"Wow, so he's considered an entrepreneur then," said Zoe.

"Yes, but probably not what you're thinking," replied Jade. "He actually sells expensive artwork."

"Oh, you're right! I didn't think that," replied Zoe.

"Well, Tony owns an art gallery also and not just one, but a couple, and he's working on a third."

"Wow, girly, get out of here!" Sasha yelled. "That explains it all!"

"So, you two have something in common: You're both lovers of art," Zoe replied.

"Yes, we are," Jade answered and smiled. "However, it's so interesting that Blaine loves art too," Jade said.

"That's right. He owns a gallery too," said Sasha.

"Wow, that is interesting," Zoe agreed.

"Ah, girly, that's so romantic. It sounds like a love story," Sasha teased.

"Okay, well, I really need to snap out of this love zone now and get some things done before I have to leave." Jade continued to work.

"Yes, there is a lot to do, so we can be ready for our big fall-wear launch. September will be here before you know it, and designers are preparing for shipping as we speak," said Zoe.

"You're right. Let's get working, girlies," said Sasha as she went to the back to get a box of hangers. Zoe walked over and checked the client book while Jade made a call to one of the designers in Paris.

Time went by, and the boutique was prepared to close for the night. Jade left before Sasha and Zoe and headed toward her Benz. She suddenly noticed a man coming in the opposite direction. Right before Jade approached her vehicle, she recognized the stranger. "Jade, is that you?" he asked in a deep, wondering voice.

"Blaine?" she asked.

"Yes," he answered at a slight distance. The two walked closer until they could see one another more clearly.

"Jade, baby, how are you?" he asked while giving her a big hug and kiss on the cheek. "Look at you!" he said excitedly while taking a step back to check her out in full view.

"I've been doing good, Blaine, and you?" Jade questioned him with amazement and the look of shock all over her face. "What brings you on this side of town?"

"Do you really want to know?"

"Yes, I do," Jade replied and walked closer to Blaine. She hoped to hear a response her heart could take, considering their history. Jade first heard a deep sigh.

"Okay, I was missing you and needed to see your face again, so I thought to stop by the boutique to pay you a visit. I guess my timing was a little off, but hey, I did catch you before you actually left," Blaine replied and reached his hands toward hers.

"Oh, I see. Well, here I am, and yes, I must admit it's good to see you too—a little overwhelming and a pleasant surprise."

"Yeah, it's been a little while since we last conversed, but you've constantly been on my mind. Although I'm moving on with my life, I still see visions of your gorgeous face, and I just wanted to reach out and grab for you."

Jade was at a loss for words after a glance in those mysterious eyes of his. She then remembered how Blaine used to make her feel. At that point, Blaine politely took her hand. Then Jade immediately snapped back from her thoughts. With her purse and laptop bag in her free hand, she decided to scramble for her keys. "I should have had these out already." Jade shook her head.

"It's okay, babe. I'm pretty sure you would have if I hadn't shown up out-of-the-blue," said Blaine.

"Yes, you're absolutely right. Normally I take my keys out before I approach my car, so I'll be ready to just get in."

He then noticed Jade struggling. "Here, let me help you with that." Blaine opened her back door so she could put her bag in.

"Thanks. That's really kind of you," said Jade, cracking a little grin. She immediately laid her bag on the backseat and looked back in his direction.

"Well, you should know by now that that's just the way I am. My mother raised me to be a gentleman, and by the way, she asked about you the other day. I told her I hadn't spoken with you in a little while now."

"Really? That's sweet of her. Please tell her I said hello the next time you two talk," replied Jade.

"Will do, and she'll be glad we spoke too. You know, my mom was hoping we'd get married. She was so disappointed when I told her you said no."

Jade looked up at Blaine. "You know, it wouldn't have worked out between us due to your career. Your job responsibilities are so demanding at times," said Jade.

"You know the good ole saying, 'When duty calls'," Blaine responded and gave her a guilty sad look, "But Jade, baby—"

"No need to explain," she said and stopped him before he could finish his sentence. "Well, I must admit I was heartbroken after you proposed, but as you know, I've moved on. Tony and I are still together, and I'm happy with him." Jade slowly turned her face from his.

"Yeah, I kinda figured that you two were still seeing one another, but, of course, that wasn't going to stop me from seeing how you're doing." Blaine bluntly turned Jade back around to face him.

"You still have that determined way about you," she said. "Nothing stops Blaine from doing what Blaine wants to do," said Jade with a chuckle.

"Well, what can I say…? I know I had a good thing, but I'm also aware that you love him."

"Yes, I do, and he loves me too."

"How could he not? You're beautiful, inside-and-out, and a great mom. By the way, how are the kids?" Blaine asked as he changed the subject.

"They're good. Still out of town with Tyler."

"That's nice, and how is Mr. Jayden?" asked Blaine with a curious look as he eagerly waited for the response.

"Oh, he's fine. Hasn't changed much. Still a little big-headed," Jade answered.

Blaine shook his head. "Glad it's going good on your end," he said softly.

"Yes, it is, and thanks for your concern." Jade responded rather quickly to stop any emotions from forming.

"Oh, you know I have to make sure my baby is okay," said Blaine.

"Your baby?" Jade questioned. "Blaine, I'm not single anymore, and you really have to start accepting it." Jade said as she kindly corrected him.

"Okay… you're right, and I will. Well, I do. It's just that I love you, and sometimes, I feel as though I owe you so much. Or, should I say, there's so much more I wish to have given you."

"Blaine, you don't owe me anything. It was good when we were together. You just didn't have the time to fully dedicate to the relationship, so please don't beat yourself up about it. I understood the situation," Jade said, reassuring him that she was all right now.

Blaine walked closer to her and kissed her forehead. "Have dinner with me tonight," he suggested.

"I can't. We have a new line to prepare for, and I don't want to stay out late. Also, it wouldn't be a good idea since I'm in a relationship with Tony now," Jade explained.

"Yeah, I guess you're right," he said. "I understand, baby. You have to get your beauty rest, so I'll let you get going. It was good seeing you again, but know if he ever messes up, I'm going after him."

Jade shook her head and got in her vehicle. "You are too much," she said and closed the door.

"No, I care, that's all." Blaine leaned in to kiss Jade, but she quickly turned her face and the kiss landed on her cheek.

"You take care yourself, Blaine," Jade said after starting her vehicle.

"You do the same," he responded and tapped the hood of Jade's Mercedes as he walked off. Jade put on her seatbelt, adjusted the rear mirror, and drove away.

6

Tony went out of town on business.

It was 5 a.m. when Jade heard her phone ringing.

"Who in the world is calling me this early?" she grumbled and removed the eye mask from her eyes then reached to grab the phone off the nightstand. "Tony?" she said in question, barely able to read the caller's name. "What in God's earth is he calling me so early for? He knows I'm not up at this time of the morning."

"Good morning, baby. Is everything okay?" she asked, struggling to get her words out.

"Yes, babe. Everything is fine, but I needed to tell you that I have to leave town this morning. One of the managers at the gallery in Cali has to discuss some business with me regarding a few new art pieces that he wants to bring in. These are some very expensive paintings, and, of course, this type of business should not be discussed over the phone," Tony kindly explained.

"I see," Jade responded in her sleepy voice. "How long will you be gone?" she asked, sounding a bit disappointed.

"Until Friday evening," Tony answered. "I'm going to have my pilot fly me out this morning, so I can have all that taken care of and get back," he added.

"Well, I think I'll be okay for a couple of days, but no longer than that," Jade said, lying back on the bed.

"You got it, baby," Tony replied. "Hey, how about dinner Friday evening? I'll have my driver pick you up from your house. Let's say around 7?" he excitedly asked.

"That sounds good, babe," Jade answered, still sounding as if she was not fully awake. "So, what would my handsome man like me to wear?"

"Oh, I'm pretty sure you can find something nice in that huge collection of yours," he responded with a chuckle.

"Yes, I'm quite sure I can," said Jade, "and since you didn't suggest anything, I'll assume you're leaving it up to me."

Tony got quiet for a few seconds and reflected on the real plans he had for Jade when he returned. Being disturbed by the silence, Jade called out to him, "Babe, are you still there?"

After snapping out of his thoughts, he answered, "Yes, babe, I'm here. Wear something really nice," he expressed in a soft tone.

"Okay, something really nice it is. I have just the dress," Jade replied, thinking about one of the new dresses that came into the boutique last week.

"Jade, baby, one last thing: I love you," he said unexpectedly.

"Tony, my love, I know you do, and I love you too," she responded. "Well, shouldn't you get going, babe?"

"Yes!" he answered quickly after looking at the time on his black Rolex. "You have a great day. I'll call you later, and Jade, babe, don't work too hard."

"I'll try not to, but you, on the other hand, be safe," she said and looked at the clock on her nightstand.

"Thanks, and I can't wait to see you when I get back!" Tony said and hung up the phone.

Jade ended the call and laid the phone down on the bed. After a short sigh and a much-needed stretch, she decided that it was time to get up. Jade said her morning prayers and headed to the bathroom to take a shower. "Lord, could this be the man I've prayed for?" she asked softly then reached for a shower cap. "You know, Lord, the kind of man that would love me and my children? And if so, please let me not mess this up by going there too soon. You know, Lord, how we do sometimes." She stepped in the shower, grabbed her favorite shower gel, closed the glass door, and began to wash.

It was around 9 a.m. when Jade arrived at the boutique wearing denim skinny jeans, a white designer t-shirt, a black blazer, and her favorite pair of wedge heels. No one else was in the boutique, so she turned on all the lights.

"What is this?" Jade was displeased with the new shoe line one of her designers had sent. "Do they really expect us to sell these? We are a classy boutique—not some tasteless place!" Jade tossed the shoe on the counter. "Lord, forgive me, but they know I don't carry nothing but the best lines in my boutique." Within seconds, she was calling Sasha.

The phone rang and Sasha answered. "Hola, chica. How's my sis on this beautiful morning?"

Jade took a deep breath before speaking. "Hello Sasha. I could be better."

"What's wrong?" Sasha asked.

"I'm at the boutique looking at the new shoes they sent us, and I am not happy."

"Yes, Zoe told me how they looked, and she said you would not be pleased."

"No, I'm not, and they're supposed to go on the shelf tomorrow for sale. By the way, where is Zoe? I'd figured she must have opened the shipment, but the lights were off when I walked in this morning. It's almost 10 a.m., and I still don't see her," said Jade before Sasha could get a word in.

"Oh, she called and told me that she had to run out before the boutique opened. Something she needed to take care of before work. She'd mentioned you were coming in around 9:30 this morning and that she'll be back by 10:00," Sasha explained.

"Yes, I'm here, but she needs to hurry so we can figure out what we're going to do with these shoes," said Jade.

"I agree, girly," Sasha said and checked the time on her phone. "I will be there shortly myself."

"Okay, you go ahead and get ready while I look online at the order to see what happened," Jade said and then opened her laptop.

"Sure thing, chica. See you soon," Sasha said and ended the call. Jade went online to the check out their order and noticed they mistakenly sent a wrong style.

Zoe walked in quickly with a bag in one hand and a cappuccino in the other. She rushed to put her things down to see what was going on. "Good morning, Jade. Sorry I'm a little late, but I had to leave to take care of something. I'm here now though," Zoe added. Jade was silent while she looked over the order that came from Paris. "Oh, you saw those not-so-cute shoes they sent us," said Zoe as she glanced at the order.

Jade nodded her head. "Yes, and I see where they were supposed to send us this style." She pointed to the stylish heels on their website. "Okay, Zoe, I need you to call Ms. Pino in Paris. Tell her what happened, and see how fast we can have these in our boutique. ASAP, Zoe!" Jade yelled.

"Yes, ma'am, I'm on it!" Zoe politely yelled back.

"By the way, good morning, and thanks for your help."

Zoe smiled and began dialing Ms. Pino. Jade took a walk around the boutique, making sure everything else was in place and ready for today's business. She went over near the jewelry and spotted a beautiful gold bracelet. "Hmmm… this would look really nice with the dress I'm thinking about wearing to dinner tonight when Tony returns." Jade picked up the bracelet and tried it on. While looking at it on her wrist in the mirror, Jade nodded her head up and down. "Yes, I am getting this today. It goes perfect with my dress," she quietly whispered then went to the counter to package it for purchase. "Okay, everything else is good, and we're ready for business," Jade said and put her bracelet aside.

"Alright, it's done! The heels are being prepared for today's shipment and should be here in three days!" Zoe said excitedly.

"Three days?" Jade questioned. "I guess, but that should've happened in the first place. Our clients know we come number one in customer service. They are expecting to see all of the new line, not part of it, but… oh well. Let's just pray for a great day and that business goes well."

"I agree," replied Zoe.

"Okay, where's Ms. Sasha? Our clients can walk in the door any time now," said Jade.

"Well… speak of the angel!" said Zoe.

"¡Hola, chicas! How's everything?" Sasha asked and went over to put her purse and coffee down.

"Hi, Sasha," Zoe responded.

"Hello, Sasha," Jade replied shortly after.

"Girly, what did you decide to do about the ugly shoe syndrome?" asked Sasha. "I know we are not putting those on the shelf."

"No, Zoe took care of it. Ms. Pino is sending us the correct style, and we must prepare to ship the wrong ones back," Jade responded.

"Gladly!" shouted Zoe.

"Thanks, hon. The rest are still in the box," said Jade.

"So, girly, what's new with you and Mr. Lover Man?" Sasha asked and chuckled.

Zoe looked up from packing the boxes. "Yes, how's Tony doing?"

"Well, Tony is good. He called me early this morning to tell me he's going out of town on business," Jade answered.

"Okay, and how do you feel about that? I mean, are you okay with him leaving with such short notice?" asked Zoe.

"Yeah, girly, that's the stuff Blaine used to do. He was always talking about going away for a few days on business," Sasha added.

"Oh, no, ladies. Tony's only gone for about two and half days. He assured me that he's only going because this business can't be discussed over the phone, and he needed to approve the artwork," Jade explained. "I know. It sounded a little familiar when he told me, but I'm alright with it. He doesn't go often, and besides, it's just for a couple of days," she added.

"Okay, girly. As long as you're good, we're good," said Sasha, and then she looked at Jade.

"That's right," Zoe added.

"Yes, I'm good. Thank you. The one I'm a bit concerned about is Blaine," Jade said and walked over to the window.

"Blaine? Why Blaine? I thought you two were done," said Zoe.

"Yeah, girly, so what's going on with Blaine now?" asked Sasha.

"Oh, it's nothing going on with us, which is why I'm concerned," answered Jade. "I believe he's having a bit of a struggle trying to cope with us not being together anymore. Sometimes Blaine crosses my mind, and I wonder how's he's doing, what he's up to, and if he's still in town, or gone back on one of his job missions."

"Jade, dear, Blaine will be fine. You go on and be happy with Tony," said Zoe, then she walked over to where Jade was standing.

"Yes, girly, you and Tony are good together, and I've never seen you happier," Sasha said.

"You're right," said Jade, "but the thing is, we didn't break up on bad terms. It was because he didn't have enough time for the relationship. I really wanted it to work, but he didn't enough, well, that's what it seemed like. His job got between us, and only his job. He loved me, and y'all know I loved him," Jade explained.

"Yes, we knew." Sasha touched Jade on her shoulder. "Well, just pray, girly, that he moves on with his life and allows you to move on with yours," said Sasha.

"Pray?" yelled Jade and Zoe at the same time. Then they looked at Sasha in shock.

"You said 'pray'!" Zoe teased.

"Ahh, yeah… I pray. I love the Lord, too, and besides, I've been attending church services this month," Sasha responded.

Zoe and Jade looked at one another again then at Sasha. "That's good, Sasha," said Zoe.

"Yes, it is," Jade added. They both ran over to give her a hug. "We know you love the Lord, and He loves you too. We're just messing with you, hon," said Jade.

"Yeah," Zoe agreed. Then the two of them started laughing.

"You chicas are something else, but I love you both. Okay, so how did we get on me? I thought we were talking about Jade," said Sasha as she started placing a few pairs of the new heels on the display wall.

"Yes, we were, but that was too cute," Jade responded with a smile. "Oh, by the way, Tony is taking me to dinner when he returns. I'm to be ready by 7 p.m. on Friday evening. He's having his driver pick me up, and I'm going to meet him at the restaurant."

"Wow, girly, that sounds nice. Which restaurant this time? One on the other side of the world?" Sasha asked teasing Jade.

"No, girl. But the funny thing is that I really don't know which one this time. All I know is to wear a really nice dress as per the Mr.'s request," Jade added.

"When have you ever known?" Zoe questioned.

"Right." They all agreed and laughed together.

"Well, I'll just do what the Mr. says, and hope it'll be a wonderful night as always," said Jade as she gazed out the window.

"We have clients coming in," said Zoe and quickly made sure her hair was in place.

"You take the first, and I'll take the second client," said Sasha as she walked to greet the people coming in the boutique. "Welcome," she said and began assisting them.

Meanwhile, Jade went in the back to check out the stockroom, making sure everything was clean. She then decided to take a look at her phone to see if there was a missed call or text. She immediately saw a text from the kids. It read: *We miss you, Mom. Hope we can video chat soon* with three heart shapes. She responded: *Mommy loves you, too, and yes, we can video chat soon… I can't wait. Love, Mom.* Jade hit send and attempted to place her phone down, but it began ringing.

"Tony!" she softly yelled while trying to hurry up and answer the call. "Hello, Tony, babe, is this you?" Jade said.

"Yes, it's me, baby. I wanted to tell you I'm almost at the gallery. I was sitting here in the car thinking about you, and well, I also wanted to hear your voice," Tony explained.

"No need for an explanation. I love you too," Jade said and positioned herself more comfortably. "I guess our selfie just isn't enough, huh?" she asked smiling.

"Nope, I wanted to hear your voice too. I just miss you. Well, baby, I hope your day continues to go good, but I'm going to have to hop off here now," said Tony and glanced out the window. He then began to wonder how Jade was going to react to his surprise.

"Right, I understand," Jade replied. "Oh, I received a text from the kids, and they want to video chat with me."

Tony laughed. "That's nice. You should."

"What's so funny?" Jade asked.

"How you said video chat like you're a youngster or something. But, oh yeah… I know they miss their mom some kind of terrible," he added.

"Yes, they do, and I'll be sure to mention you too. I know the kids can't wait to meet you in person instead of over the computer!" Jade said excitedly.

"Yes, I can't wait either. Okay, baby, I'm going now. I'll reach out to you again soon. Love you, Jade," Tony said and ended the call.

Jade began working on some important paperwork while Sasha and Zoe worked the floor. She hoped that the sales were good today even though she worked in the back office for most of the afternoon and into the evening.

It was close to 6:30 p.m. Zoe and Sasha began tallying up the sales for the day. Jade wrapped up her work then headed out to the front. "Hey, ladies, how did we do today?" asked Jade.

"Well, with the new line, we did good, but I know if we had those bad new heels that everyone's wearing in Paris, we'd have done even better," replied Zoe.

"Yes, girly, everyone was asking about those shoes, and I just told them to come back this weekend. We'll have them then," said Sasha and pulled her hair back into a ponytail and fanned her face.

"Yeah, she's right. I had a few ask me as well," said Zoe and started straightening the jeans table. "They would have been a hit."

"Oh, I could imagine, and they probably wondered why we didn't have them as we said," Jade said disappointedly.

"Only a few customers questioned, and the rest just went about their regular shopping," said Sasha.

"They know it had to really be something if we didn't have an item when we said," Zoe added.

"That's right, girly. We are the #1 Boutique in New York!" Sasha yelled then walked over to help Zoe with the jeans.

"I love you two, and that's what makes us a great team," Jade replied and grabbed her belongings. "Well, ladies, I'm going to get ready to head out now. I have a video chat appointment with my kids tonight."

"Oh, that's nice," said Zoe and walked towards her.

"Yes, I know, and I can't wait to see their cute faces. I miss them so much," Jade added.

"I bet you do, girly," Sasha said as she began to walk toward the two of them.

"Okay, well, you need to get going then," Zoe encouraged Jade.

"Alright, goodnight, ladies," Jade said.

"Goodnight, and tell the kids we said hello," they both said and waved bye.

"I sure will!" Jade yelled before closing her car door and driving off.

Jade pulled up in front of her building after a nice, relaxing drive from the boutique. "Hey there, Mr. Franklin! How's my favorite man?" Jade asked after she got out the car so Sean could park it. "Okay, Sean, he's all yours! But be careful with him because I know you get happy when I let you park my baby."

"Yes, ma'am!" Sean said and smiled. He quickly jumped in the driver's seat of Jade's vehicle and drove off.

"Mr. Franklin, I spoke to you. Didn't you hear me? Is everything alright, Mr. Franklin? You look a little down today." Jade stood in front of him waiting for a response.

"Oh, I'm okay, pretty lady," Mr. Franklin said as he opened the door for one of the other residents.

"Ah, I don't know. You don't seem like your cheerful self today, and I want to know what's going on," Jade said, demanding an answer.

"Alright…. this will be my last week working for you kind people. I have to be getting on. My time here is coming to an end," explained Mr. Franklin.

"Wait. I don't understand," Jade responded sadly. "You're leaving us for another location?" she asked, trying to gain clarity.

"No, pretty lady. I'm hanging up my uniform. I'm done working. Gonna retire now. It's about that time; heck, I've been at this building for about fifteen years!" Mr. Franklin explained.

"Oh my, Mr. Franklin, I don't know what to say other than you're the best-of-the-best, and you'll be greatly missed," Jade said expressively.

"Okay, now, don't go getting all mushy on me. You and the kids can visit me as often as you like. I'll be sure to leave my contact information at the office," he said, trying to cheer Jade up.

"Okay, you do that, and we'll make it our duty to come check on you," Jade replied. She gave Mr. Franklin a hug.

"Alright, you have yourself a good night, pretty lady, and tell those kids of yours I said hello."

"Will do." Jade went in the building and waited for the next elevator. When she arrived at her floor, she opened her door to her place and put her purse and bag down on the couch. *Ah, so good to be home.* Jade opened a bottled water and pulled her laptop out of her bag. Looking at the time, she saw that it was almost 8 p.m. "Oh, dear, I don't want them to think I forgot," Jade said as she waited for the internet connection to load.

Jayden picked up the call. "Mommy!" he yelled after seeing her face.

"Hi, Jayden, how's my big boy?" she happily asked.

"I'm fine, Mommy, and where's Skittles? Let me see Skittles!" Jayden yelled excitedly.

"Sure," Jade said. She called for Skittles to come while Jayden excitedly called for Brittany.

"Brittany! Come here and see Mommy and Skittles."

Brittany ran over near Jayden and saw her mom and Skittles in the background. "Mommy, I miss you!" she said as she put her face closer to the computer screen.

"I miss you, too, baby. I miss both of you!" said Jade. "Hey, guess who else misses the both of you?"

"Who?" the kids asked.

"Auntie Zoe, Auntie Sasha, and my good friend, Tony," she replied.

"Tell them hi, and we miss them too," said Jayden. "Your boyfriend, too, Mommy…" he added with a laugh.

"Oh, okay, I will tell Tony you said hello." Jade smiled.

"Me, too, Mommy!" said Brittany, yelling in the background.

"Okay, baby. I will tell all of them! I hope you two have been good for Daddy, and where's he anyway?" asked Jade.

"He's in the living room watching TV," answered Brittany.

"Okay, tell Daddy I said hi, and I will call him soon. Alright… it's getting late, my children, and Mommy has to get ready for bed herself."

"Okay, Mommy, have good dreams, and don't let the bed bugs bite," said Jayden laughing.

"Yes, Mommy, don't let them bite you!" Brittany repeated with a laugh.

"I won't, and you two don't forget to say your prayers. Oh, and call your grandparents. I know they would love to hear your voices," she added.

"Okay, Mommy. We will call them tomorrow," said Jayden.

"Good! Alright, goodbye for now… love you," Jade said before logging off.

"Love you, too, Mommy!" They both yelled at the same time. Jade smiled and ended the call.

Jade put her laptop away, and then got herself ready for a shower. *I think a fresh pedicure is in line. Look at these toes! I'll just call in the morning to schedule an afternoon appointment. I'm sure Niecy can squeeze me in, and I'll get my nails done too. My hands have to be pretty for the evening,* she thought after looking at her fingernails. "I know Tony is going to be pleasantly pleased when he lays eyes on me," Jade said.

Jade walked over to the shower. She began singing one of her favorite songs while she washed up. Due to the loudness of the water, she missed the new text alert sound from her cell phone. It was from her brother, Zack, over in France. Approximately fifteen minutes had gone by when Jade stepped out the shower. She first dried her hair then her body.

"Did I miss a call?" Jade questioned and walked over to look at her phone. "No, it's a text from Zack!" Jade said with excitement. "I wonder what he's talking about," she thought and read the message. "Oh, good! He wants to plan a visit but needs to know when I'll have some free time," Jade said excitedly then tied her satin robe closed.

Jade quickly grabbed her phone and began texting back: *Hey there, Zack; how's my big brother? Sure, I would love for you to come visit. I actually can't wait, and I know the kids will love to see you too. As for me having free time, well, that's kind of funny because lately I haven't had much; but I can definitely make time for my big brother! Let's look at the end of next month.* She hit send and got herself comfortable on her bed.

She grabbed the book off her nightstand and began reading where she'd left off. As she was reading her book, another text message came in from Zack. His reply was: *Okay, Sis, we'll try for next month. I'll be in touch soon, so we can finalize everything. Bye for now. Love you!*

"Now, where was I?" Jade asked. She found where she'd left off and read for about a half hour before another text message came through. At that point, Jade was getting sleepy and had prepared to go to bed. *Okay, who is this now?* She wondered.

Jade managed to get her phone but struggled to open her eyes to read the message. "It's from Tony," Jade said, barely able to get her words out. She then put the phone close to her face to read the message. It said: *Good night, my lovely lady. Know that I love you and look forward to seeing your pretty face soon.* Jade cracked a small smile then replied back: *Tony, my love, I can't wait to see you either. I hope all is going well so far… going to bed now. Goodnight… kisses!* She hit send, laid her phone on the nightstand, and fell asleep.

It was around 7 a.m. when Jade got up and began her regular routine. All she could think was, *One more day before Tony comes home. So much to do in such little time. Guess I should call Niecy to make my appointment for tomorrow afternoon.* Jade reached for her phone. She then scrolled through her contacts, touched "salon" and placed the call.

"Hello, Classy Lady Salon. This is Niecy."

"Hi Niecy, this is Jade. How are you this morning?" Jade asked.

"Oh, hey, Jade. I'm good, hon. What can I do for you? Wait, let me guess." Niecy said before Jade could answer. "Your man is taking you out somewhere special, and you need your hair done, right?"

Jade shook her head then smiled. "Yes, Niecy, you're right. Tony is taking me out tomorrow evening, and I have to look really nice."

"I knew it!" shouted Niecy. "You got it. Let me see what I have for this evening, or would you like tomorrow afternoon instead?"

"Well, I was thinking to get a manicure and pedicure also. So, how about tomorrow afternoon? That way, everything will be nice and fresh," answered Jade.

"Yes, I agree. Tomorrow afternoon it is. Let's say around 1 p.m., leaving you enough time to go home and get all dolled up for your man," said Niecy.

"You're the best!" Jade shouted. "I will see you on tomorrow then. Have a good day," she added before ending the call.

"You, too, hon," Niecy replied and hung up the phone.

"Okay, that's out of the way," Jade said. She walked over near the kitchen, poured Skittles some puppy food, and filled her bowl with water. "Now, for my jog," Jade said and grabbed a bottled water from the refrigerator. She walked over to the table to get her waist pouch. She quickly bent over to tighten her shoelaces, peaked in the mirror to straighten her ponytail, then headed out the door. After her elevator ride down, she arrived at the front of the building.

"Morning, Mr. Franklin," Jade said and took off jogging down the street.

"Good morning, Ms. Jade," he replied and waved his hand while he watched her run off.

About five minutes later, Jade approached a traffic light and was forced to slow down. She decided to listen to some music and took out her earphones. Quickly, Jade placed them in her ear, touched play, and took off running again. Jade continued jogging for about thirty minutes until all of a sudden, she decided to visit the fine art gallery, which was around the corner: the one she loved so dearly and which happened to be one that Tony owned.

"Yes, I'll swing by there to see some of the new pieces. It's such a beautiful day, and what better way to enjoy it?" Jade said and crossed over to the other side of the street.

As she approached the gallery, Jade noticed a shiny, black vehicle parked in front. After Jade entered through the door, she looked back at the nice-looking vehicle. "Now that's one clean ride," she said under her breath and continued toward the guard's desk.

Jade smiled at the guard as usual then headed in to view the newest pieces first. As she got closer to the paintings, Jade saw a crowd standing around one art piece in particular. *It's pretty early for a crowd like this,* she thought as she moved in closer to see the work of art herself.

At that point, Jade, too, was in awe at what she saw hanging on the wall. "Oh, I see why everyone is over here. That's a remarkable piece, and so unique. I wonder who painted it!" she questioned with excitement. Then she squeezed through the crowd to see the name at the bottom of the painting. It read "Don Pierre" in fancy cursive lettering. While Jade was admiring the painting, she noticed a man standing next to her. *He looks very important,* Jade thought and took a quick glance at his shoes, then at his attire, which was a dark gray designer suit. *Definitely tailor-made because it fits him so perfectly,* she thought.

Jade then decided to stop looking at the man and focused back on the art hanging on display.

"Hello," he said, kindly interrupting her study. Jade wasn't sure if he was speaking to her or not, so she just ignored him and continued admiring the art. "Hello," the man kindly said again, making his accented voice more noticeable.

This time, Jade looked his way and spoke back. "Hello," she politely said then quickly focused back on the painting.

"It's a real beauty," the man said as if he knew paintings.

"Yes, it is quite a work of art," Jade replied in a soft tone.

"You come here often?" the man asked. "I see you have an eye for great work." His eyes then roamed around the gallery, noticing other nice pieces.

"Yes, I do," Jade said very briefly, "and I must admit the painter has tremendous skills and is extremely talented."

"I must agree," the man responded, slightly looking in Jade's direction. "I'm sorry. I didn't get your name," he said and held out his hand.

"Oh, it's Jade," she said, extending her hand to his. They then greeted each other with a casual handshake. "I didn't get your name either," Jade said to the man.

"You can call me Don," he replied with a smile.

"Well, nice to meet you, Don," she said bashfully and began walking away, leaving him standing there alone.

"Did you just finish jogging?" he kindly asked just before she left his side.

"Oh, me? Yes," Jade answered and looked down at her workout gear. "It's such a nice day out; plus, I saw the gallery and thought to walk in to see what's new," she explained.

"Looks like you made the right choice. As for me, I'm just here on business. I'm not from what you call the big city," Don said and smiled.

"Clearly. Your accent is too strong. Let me guess: London, right?" Jade said then looked up at Don.

"Wow, you're good. Yes, beautiful, London is correct."

"Well, Don, it was really nice meeting you, but I must get going," she said and prepared herself to leave for a second time.

"Yes, I understand. It was most pleasurable meeting you today, Jade." Don reached in his pocket. Jade smiled and headed toward the exit door. "Excuse me, Jade. Can I please give you this?" he asked and handed her a business card.

"Oh, sure," she said and extended her hand out to accept it. Don smiled and slowly turned back toward the painting. Jade looked at the business card and read what was written on the front in fancy, bold letters: *CEO-Artist Don Pierre and International Business of Fine Art.*

"Wait a minute!" Jade said and immediately stopped walking. "No way! He's the painter of that fine piece of art on the wall," she said in amazement. "It just can't be," Jade said quietly then immediately turned around to go back to find out if it's true, but when she walked in the room, there was no Don. They had somehow missed each other due to the crowd of people in the gallery, so she decided to see if he was outside and saw that the black, shiny truck had pulled off.

"He's gone," Jade said disappointedly and placed the card in her pouch. "Just wait until I tell the ladies this! Oh, but I have to tell Tony also," she said and pulled out her phone. "Okay, but who do I tell first?" she questioned then immediately touched "boutique" to call Zoe and Sasha.

"Hello, this is Zoe."

"Hi, Zoe. This is Jade! Where's Sasha?" she asked before Zoe could speak back.

"Hi Jade. She's on the floor. Is everything okay?" Zoe asked in concern because of Jade's fast talking and high tone.

"Yes, I'm just excited about something and wanted to share it with the both of you!"

"Oh, good. Okay, let me see if I can pull her away for few minutes," said Zoe. She then called for Sasha, "Come quick!" Zoe yelled. "It's Jade on the phone, and she has something to tell us."

Sasha held up one finger and yelled back, "I'm coming! One second, girly!" Zoe got back on the phone and told Jade she was coming. Soon after, Sasha ran over to where Zoe was standing and yelled, "What is going on?"

Zoe shrugged her shoulders, put the phone on speaker and said, "We're here."

"Okay, good!" Jade answered excitedly. "Now, you ladies know I went jogging this morning?"

"Yes…" replied Zoe.

"But what you didn't know is that I decided to walk in the gallery." "Girly, that's nothing new though," said Sasha.

"Yeah, you go there all the time," Zoe added.

"Right, I do, but this time, something amazing happened," Jade said. "Really?" Sasha questioned then looked at Zoe.

"Yes, I met the most mysterious, handsome man today—aside from my Tony, that is," Jade quickly added with a smile.

"Okay, okay, and what else?" Zoe anxiously asked.

"Well, the way it all happened reminded me of a movie or something," Jade said. "I was standing in the showroom where all the new masterpieces are placed. As I stood admiring one piece of art in particular, a man was admiring the same artwork."

"What's so mysterious about that?" asked Sasha.

"Right?" Zoe added.

"No… no, that's not it!" Jade said excitedly. "It's who he was. Well, I believe he was," Jade said.

"What? Girly?" questioned Sasha.

"I know it sounds a little confusing," Jade responded. "Let me finish," she added. "Okay, so, I had a brief conversation with this man about the beautiful art piece displayed in the showcase. By the way, did I mention how handsome he was, standing all tall next to me?" Jade questioned.

"Yes, yes, now go on," said Zoe.

"Okay, this is where it gets good and why I call him mysterious," said Jade. "When I was about to leave, he offered me one of his business cards. Of course, I accepted and began reading it before I walked away. In fancy bold letters, it said, *'CEO-Artist Don Pierre and International Business of Fine Art.' Nice,* I thought and started to put the card in my pouch. Then it hit me, and I immediately took it back out and began thinking, could he be the artist that painted that new masterpiece on display?" Jade explained.

"Well, do you believe that was him?" asked Zoe.

"I don't know, girly. This just sounds like a man giving a pretty lady a business card," said Sasha.

"Wait… What was the artist's name on the painting?" asked Zoe.

"Yeah, what was the mysterious name?" asked Sasha.

"Don Pierre," Jade answered. "That's the name that was written at the bottom of the painting."

"Oh…" said Zoe and Sasha at the same time.

"Plus, he was humbly knowledgeable of that piece and expressed a love for it as I did," Jade added.

"Well, are you going to call him?" asked Zoe

"Call him for what?" Jade asked.

"To see if he painted the artwork at the gallery," answered Sasha.

"Hmmm… I don't know," said Jade. "It would feel kind of weird; plus, what would I say?" she asked.

"Something would come to you, but you should find out if it's really him," said Zoe.

"Okay, but what about Tony? He probably wouldn't like the idea of me calling a man that gave me his card," Jade replied.

"Are you going to tell Tony about this mysterious man you met?" asked Zoe.

"Yes, I had thought to tell him also," answered Jade. "Besides, I did meet him at his art gallery, and it's not like any wrong gestures were made. He was very professional about it."

"Yeah, girly, but from the sound of it, the man was fine!" Sasha said jokingly. Zoe quickly tapped her arm, shook her head, then chuckled.

"Well, I've talked to handsome men before. This was all innocent, and I know my babe. He'll be glad I shared my experience with him. You ladies are too much!" said Jade and shook head.

"I'm just teasing, girly, but see if he's single though," said Sasha.

"For what?" asked Jade.

"I don't know. Just in case Mike messes up, then I can date me a rich painter," Zoe tapped her arm and shook her head again.

"No, I'm not seeing if he's single, and I'm getting ready to hop off this phone," said Jade. "Before I go, Zoe, please see how many boxes of accessories we have in stock, then text me the total so I'll have an idea of what's left," Jade added.

"Will do," said Zoe.

"Oh, and Sasha, you know better than trying to have a man on the side." "You mean a Plan B," said Zoe.

"Yeah, whatever it's called," Jade said.

"I was just playing, girly. I love me some Mike," Sasha replied and slightly rolled her head. Zoe laughed.

Jade chuckled then looked at the time. "Okay, chat soon, ladies." Jade ended the call and jogged back home to take a shower.

When Jade arrived back at her condo, it was around midday. She rushed through the double doors to her apartment building and headed to the elevator. When she approached her floor, Jade kindly spoke to the neighbors that passed in the hallway. She entered her condo, slipped her feet out her sneakers, and began undressing in the living room.

Afterwards, Jade started the shower. Skittles followed behind and sat next to Jade's bed. Meanwhile, Jade hung her pouch on a closet hook, walked over, and closed the window shades before getting in the shower. The time had begun to go by after a long, relaxing shower.

"I feel refreshed," Jade said as she flopped on the bed and positioned herself comfortably. "I should look at our inventory roster," she thought out loud and flipped open her laptop. "That shower was just what I needed," she said before reviewing the list of items in stock at the boutique.

Jade sat working for about an hour before she started getting sleepy. *A nap is surely in line right about now,* she thought and closed her laptop. "I will have the ladies order some more hats tomorrow," she said and laid back on the bed and shut her eyes.

As the evening approached, Jade was still sound asleep. The phone rang and woke her up from about a two-hour-long nap. "Hello," she softly muttered, "This is Jade."

"Jade, babe, this is Tony. Are you sleeping?" he asked.

"Oh, hi, babe. Yes, I was just taking a little nap, but I'm glad to hear your voice as always," Jade replied softly and propped her head up on the pillow.

"Well, you know, I had to call and see how my number one love is doing," said Tony.

Jade smiled. "Yes, I know. So, how are things going for you out there in sunny California?"

"Business is good. Thank you. And how are things at the boutique?" Tony asked.

"Busy, but good also," replied Jade.

"What are Zoe and Sasha up to? I know they're keeping you going," he chuckled.

"Well, that's just them being them," Jade replied and chuckled too.

"Hey, by the way, I can't wait to see you."

"Neither can I," she replied. "Oh, before I forget… I have to tell you about my interesting experience at the gallery today."

"Really now?" questioned Tony. "Okay, tell me all about it. My ears are all yours," he said eagerly.

"Well, I stopped by the gallery to see what was new on display," Jade began.

"Was everything alright?" he asked.

"Yes, it's nothing like that," answered Jade.

"Cool, go on," said Tony.

"You know how when you put a new masterpiece on display, I like to see it?"

"Yes, but that's nothing new, babe. You've been doing that long before we met," said Tony.

"True, but this time it was a little different."

"Okay, how so?" asked Tony.

"I met someone there," answered Jade.

"Really? And who might this someone be?" asked Tony.

"Well, he gave me one of his business cards."

"He?" questioned Tony.

"Yes, it was a man: A very distinguished one at that," Jade answered.

"So, what did the card say on it?"

"It read 'Don Pierre'," Jade answered.

"Don? Really? You met Don P.?" Tony excitedly questioned.

"You know him?"

"Do I know him? Of course! He is one of my top artists. His pieces are beyond extraordinary! He's very well-known in his country and very wealthy too," Tony explained.

"So, he is the painter!" Jade yelled. "I knew it; well, I thought he could have been."

"Wait, he didn't introduce himself as the artist?" Tony said.

"No, and he left like some mystery man before I could even ask."

"Interesting," Tony replied. "But it does kind of sound like him: mysterious and very humble."

"You can say that again," Jade said. "Okay, so, after I saw he was gone, I thought to look outside, but the black vehicle I assumed was his was also gone."

"Yeah, he probably was in town and wanted to stop by to see how his piece was doing. It's been years since he's visited New York's gallery."

"I see… well, he was quite the gentleman and nicely dressed, I must say," Jade replied.

"Oh, of course! He wears nothing but the best-tailored attire. His suits are nothing to mess with!" Tony said with enthusiasm. "A good man to do business with, I must add."

"Well, then, mystery solved!" Jade said excitedly. "I have to tell the ladies I was correct about Mr. Pierre." She chuckled.

"So, let's hear it. Did you think he was handsome?" Tony asked.

"What did you just ask me?"

"You heard me right. Did you?" Tony asked again and eagerly waited on an answer.

Jade laughed. "I can't believe you just asked me that."

"I'm waiting…" said Tony. He covered his mouth so that Jade wouldn't hear him laughing.

"Yes, he was handsome. Now, I told you. You got your answer," said Jade, sitting all the way up on the bed after she shook her head.

"Cool, now, was that so bad?" Tony jokingly asked. "I don't know why you were acting like you couldn't tell me. I'm good, babe; we're good, and I want you to know that we can talk about any and everything," he added.

"Yes, I do know that," Jade replied.

"I love you, babe," said Tony.

"I love you too," she replied.

"So, are you ready for our big date when I get back in town?"

"Of course, I am," Jade answered. "I'm always ready to see you."

"Good, because I can't wait to be in your presence again. The night I have planned will be a special one." Tony smiled with joy.

Jade slowly got off the bed, fixed her hair, then took a peek out the window. "Ah, the sun will be going down soon, and I'm feeling really hungry right about now," she said as she headed to the kitchen.

"Yeah, babe, get something in that belly of yours," Tony said jokingly. "I can't have you all skinny and stuff. You know, I like me a nice backyard," he added with a laugh.

"Ha-ha, real cute." Jade grabbed the bread to make a sandwich. "I got this over here." She laughed too.

"Okay, love. Enjoy your food, and I will call you tomorrow after I land."

"I sure will, and I can't wait to kiss those lips of yours again," replied Jade. "Neither can I."

"Love you, babe."

"Love you too," said Tony.

They ended the call, and Jade immediately started grabbing all that was needed to make her sandwich. "Tuna fish and chips it is!" she excitedly shouted. *Thanks, Mom,* she thought, *for those good sandwiches you used to make me as a child.* Then Jade began to reminisce about her childhood and how her dad used to try and teach her about cars. *Oh, was that the blues?* Jade thought, *But he was just helping me keep my old 2003 SUV running.* "Those were the days." She smiled and flicked on the television for company while she finished her sandwich.

The night passed and the morning came when Jade heard her alarm going off. After saying her morning prayers as usual, she ended it with a "Thank You, Lord. Tony comes back today." His return was on her mind all night. She jumped up, ran in the bathroom to brush her teeth, and washed her face. Jade glanced in the mirror to make sure her teeth looked white and then headed to her closet.

"It's going to be a half-day at the boutique for me today, so I can wear something comfortable," she said and scrabbled through her clothes. "This will do!" she yelled and quickly pulled out a colorful blouse and a pair of red capri pants. "Guess I'll wear my flip flops since I have an appointment to get my feet done."

After getting dressed, she quickly put her hair in a ponytail then grabbed her phone to text the kids good morning. "I'll get a cup of coffee on the way," she said after she hit send on her phone. Jade then made sure Skittles had some food and water in her bowl and headed out the door.

It was close to 10 a.m. when Jade arrived at the boutique feeling very joyful. "Good morning, good morning," she said and walked toward the register.

"What you so happy about?" asked Zoe. "No, wait, let me say it. Tony comes back today!" Zoe said excitedly before Jade could answered.

"Yup," Jade replied and smiled then went to put her purse away.

A few minutes later, Sasha walked through the door. "Hola chicas, it's a beautiful morning."

"You can say that again," said Jade, coming from the back after overhearing Sasha.

"Wow, girly, looks like you're in a good mood," said Sasha.

"Yes, I am! My babe comes back today," Jade replied.

"I know you have something nice planned for his return," said Zoe.

"Well, he actually has a special dinner lined up for us. I'm not sure of all the details, but I know he wants me to dress somewhat semi-formal," Jade replied.

"Well, let's get this day started then," said Zoe.

"Yes, I'll put the open sign in the window," Sasha said as she unlocked the door for business.

"I agree. My appointment with Niecy is at 1 p.m. this afternoon, and we have a few things to go over before then," said Jade.

"All righty now!" said Sasha and pulled her hair back from her face.

"Oh, by the way, I looked at the inventory, and we can use some more hats," said Jade. "Place an order for some of those neck scarfs that were advertised on the website too. Autumn will be approaching in a couple of months, and I want to make sure we have some in stock," she added. "By the way, I'm really thinking to do something a little different this year and get a few leather jackets to test the market." Sasha and Zoe looked at Jade in question. "Just to see how we would do with them in the boutique," Jade explained. "I know it's not our usual, but they may do well."

"It's definitely different for us, but like you said, let's do a test sale and see what happens," agreed Zoe.

"Wait, chicas, are you saying we're putting leather jackets on the sales floor?" asked Sasha.

"Yup, that's what Boss Lady said," answered Zoe.

"Okay, I guess… but, where would they go?" asked Sasha. "We've never sold leather jackets in the boutique before."

"I know. That's why we're doing it." Jade smiled and turned to greet a customer that entered the boutique. "Welcome, how can we assist you today?" she asked the fine gentleman that looked a little lost.

"Oh, good morning," he replied in a deep voice. "I'm here to pick out a gift for my fiancé's birthday."

"Well, first, let me say, you couldn't have chosen a better place to get a nice present for her," said Jade. "Now, let me ask you, what kind of taste does she have?"

"Ahhh, she has really good taste. Kind of like you," he answered. "Okay," Jade said with a smile.

Sasha looked over at them after she overheard what he said. She then shook her head at Jade, smiled, and continued working on the racks. Jade led the fine gentleman over to the dresses.

"How about a nice dress or a purse?" she asked. "Women love getting dresses and purses as gifts from their significant others. It shows them you took some time to pick the gift out," Jade added.

"Oh, yeah?" he asked.

"Yes, it shows them you pay attention to the things they wear and what you like on them. Hey, if you bought it, you must like it, right?" Jade asked the man.

"Yeah, I guess you are right, if you put it that way." He smiled.

"So, do you see anything that catches your eye?" she asked.

"Well, what about this?" he answered, holding up a teal-green, form-fitting, polyester dress with tank sleeves.

"That's cute," Jade said. "We even have a necklace that would go great with it."

"Really? Can you show it to me?"

"Sure, right this way." Jade walked him over to the jewelry section.

"This is a nice boutique you have here," the man said.

"Thank you very much." Then she went to pick out the necklace that went with the dress. "Yeah, we do pretty good here in the city,"

Jade added and walked back near the man. "I believe this is the one I had in mind." She held the necklace against the dress. "So, what you think? It's cute, right?"

"Well, I will say, you know your stuff, Ms…? Oh, sorry, I don't see a name tag on you," he said.

"It's Jade. I'm the manager."

"Well, Jade, thank you for your kind assistance. I know my fiancé is going to love this dress." He pulled out his credit card and handed it to Jade.

She took the card and walked over to the register. The man followed behind her. "So, we're putting this on your black one?" asked Jade.

"Yes, why not? I haven't used it in a little while now."

"Oh," Jade said and smiled. She finished running his credit card through the machine and handed the card back to him. "Looks like you're all set, Mr. Davidson." Jade packaged the dress with the necklace and put them in a white box. "There you go! Thanks for coming in today, and I hope your fiancé likes the dress. Do come again," she added and waved bye.

"Oh, I'm sure she will," the man said and walked out the door.

"Alright, ladies, how we looking on those orders?" Jade asked as she looked at her phone to see if she had a missed call or message.

"We're good!" Zoe yelled from the back office.

"Hey, girlies, maybe the leather jackets can go over here," Sasha said and pointed to a corner area of the boutique.

"Okay, we can put them there," Jade agreed.

"Yeah, I don't see why not," Zoe said also in agreement.

"I was just thinking. As long as the jackets are cute, stylish, and in season, we are good," Jade added.

"Yup!" Zoe said.

"True… true…" Sasha replied.

"Alright, let's do it then," said Zoe.

With her day ending, having spent the remainder of the afternoon at Niecy's, Jade set for home to rest up a bit before her date night with Tony. Jade quickly walked past Mr. Franklin as usual; this time, she waved one hand while holding a bag in the other. Mr. Franklin waved back, shook his head, and smiled. Jade then rushed to step on the elevator before the door closed.

As soon as she approached her door, a text message came through. "It must be Tony," she said after hearing the text alert, so Jade reached in her purse to see who it was. "It's Tony!" she said with excitement. She tossed her bag and purse on the couch.

She quickly opened the message and it read: *I'll be landing soon. Love you. Tony.* Jade smiled and then turned on some music. Shortly after, she rushed to the bedroom, kicked off her shoes, called for Skittles, and laid back on the bed.

"Hi baby," she said and rubbed Skittles' head. "I'm sorry I didn't speak to you when I came in." Jade put her on the bed. "Niecy really did a good job on my nails and feet." Jade held her hands out in front of her to take another look. "Uhn, I hope Tony finds me attractive tonight. Speaking of Tony, I wonder where we are going for dinner?" Jade thought, *Hmmm… that man can be so private at times, but I do love me some him.* She smoothed and patted the top of her bun.

Time started to go by. "Oh, dear, I need to put a shower cap on, so I don't mess up my pretty hairstyle," said Jade and went into the bathroom and started scrambling through her shelf. "Or should I just take a bath? Yup, a bath it is," she decided and immediately started the water. "Alright, Skittles, you be good while I get ready for my date," Jade said and rushed past her to check the time.

Considering it was already five o'clock, Jade thought, *Tony's plane should be landing in about an hour.* Jade quickly undressed, then danced her way back in the bathroom and stepped in the tub of water. "Uhmm, this feels so good and relaxing," she said and slowly adjusted her body to the temperature of the water. Jade softly laid her head back on the pillow, sinking further under the water. Shortly after she got comfortable, her thoughts drifted back to when she and Tony met. She began reminiscing about their first encounter at Ocean Seas.

"That Tony is something else," Jade said and smiled. "I'm so glad I decided to go to that dinner. I could have missed the chance to meet such a fine man." She closed her eyes. "I remember that evening like it was yesterday. That nice smelling cologne, his cute response to us saying grace," Jade softly chuckled. "Oh, and how I teased him about his ring, and not realizing what I now see as a great guy." She continued reminiscing. *Now, I look forward to his calls and seeing that handsome face of his. I'm so grateful to Sasha and Mike for introducing us to one another,* Jade thought. She then reached for her pink bath sponge and body wash and began lathering.

After she completely covered her body with soap, she heard her phone ringing in the bedroom. "I wonder who that could be," Jade said and continued washing up. *Hmmm… maybe that was Tony calling to say he's in town,"* she thought. *Well, I should hurry up.* Jade quickly rinsed the soap off her body. *I do need time to get myself all cute for my man,* she added, then she stood to get her towel and began drying off.

Jade decided to wrap the towel around herself and went in the bedroom to check her phone. It said *'Missed Call'* on the screen. "Let me see if it was my babe calling," she said and scrolled to read the name, but no name was there—just an out of state number. "Okay, I don't know who that could've been. Well, they did leave a recording." She scrolled to the message section on her phone. Jade selected play, put the phone on speaker, then laid it on the bed, and finished drying off.

"What's up, Jade? I know it wasn't too long ago since we last spoke," said Blaine in that deep, rugged voice of his. Jade suddenly paused and slowly went over to pick up her phone. She stood in shock, holding it in her hand as she continued listening to the message. "Hope you don't mind. You are still my friend, which we agreed on. This is my new number, and I wanted you to have it. Feel free to keep it." Blaine added. "Alright, you and the kids take care."

The message ended. While still in shock, Jade slowly laid her phone back on the bed. She then reached for her lotion and slowly started applying it to her body.

"Now, that was interesting," Jade said. "That man is something else," she added and shook her head. "Well, sounds like he's doing fine, and I'm definitely good. I'll just leave things as is… I need to focus on tonight," she said excitedly and glanced at the time. "I sure hope he finds a nice lady to settle down with someday."

She immediately began dressing for her and Tony's special dinner date. "Oh, no, it's a little after six!" Jade said anxiously. She rushed over to her dresser and chose a perfume to wear.

She then ran over to the closet and started looking through her purses for the best one to go with her dress. "Here's one," she said and pulled out a cute, small, black, designer patent wristlet. "Yes, this will go nice with this dress." Jade held it against her elegant, red, strappy dress that she picked out. "Tony's going to love me in this, and oh, my, the slit on the side is just perfect. It doesn't show too much thigh, but just enough peek-a-boo." She softly chuckled. "Uhmm, watch out there, now, Mr. Tony. Your lady is going to knock your socks off tonight!" Jade playfully struck a pose in her floor-length mirror.

"Okay, now, for the heels. Hmmm… decisions, decisions," she said and looked at all the shoes lined up on the shelf. "I guess I'll go with these." Jade pulled down a pair of black, patent stilettos to match her purse. "Yes, these will be perfect!" she excitedly said and walked over to the bed to sit and put on her heels.

Shortly afterwards, a text alert sounded on her phone. "Oh, dear, what time is it? That must be Tony or maybe the driver!" she said anxiously and grabbed her phone. "Let's see who it is." Jade quickly opened the text. It read: *I'm outside waiting, but please, take your time, Ms. Jade. –Driver.*

"Oh, it's Tony's driver! He's outside waiting! Am I ready?" she asked herself and took one last look in the mirror? "My makeup… I have to do my makeup!" Jade shouted and quickly grabbed her cosmetic bag and began applying a light application of makeup. "I won't do too much," she said applying a ruby red color on her lips and adding a little blush to her cheeks. "Oh, yeah, I have to bring my eyes out with a little eyeliner and shadow. Okay, that should do it," she said and puckered up her lips.

Jade lightly patted the sides of her hair and took one last look in the mirror. *Nice…,* she thought and then grabbed her wristlet and keys off the dresser and headed for the door. "Goodnight, Skittles. Mommy's leaving for a little while," Jade said after making sure she had food and water in her bowl.

Jade immediately left, locked the door, and strutted to the elevator. After reaching the lobby level in the apartment building, she noticed a man in uniform standing in front of a stretched black limo. "Hello, Ms. Jade, I've been awaiting your arrival," the man politely said.

"Hello to you, sir. I hope I didn't keep you waiting too long," she replied and smiled.

"Oh, no ma'am. We are going to make good time. Mr. Tony will be so delighted to see you," the driver said and opened the car door for Jade to get in.

"Thank you," she said as she got in the car.

Startled, Jade looked and saw that Tony was sitting in the car also. "How's my babe been doing?" he said and leaned over to kiss Jade's cheek. She couldn't believe her eyes! It was Tony sitting there next to her.

"Oh my God, babe, you're home!" Jade was so excited and quickly slid over closer to hug him. "Why didn't you tell me you were back?"

He then placed one of his hands on hers. "I wanted to surprise you… Surprise!" Tony yelled then chuckled.

Jade softly hit his leg. She chuckled too. "Well, you did just that," she said and placed one of her hands on his; then she lightly laid her head on his shoulder. After Tony and Jade got comfortable, the driver drove off and headed to their destination.

"Babe, we have some catching up to do," she said, rubbing his hand. "You can start by telling me all about your trip," Jade suggested.

Tony looked in her direction. "Well, my trip turned out to be a much-needed one. It was a good thing I went out there to discuss it in person."

"Yeah, it probably was," Jade replied. "I'm glad you took care of business, and you're back home with me," she added.

"Yes, me too, babe. I missed you those couple days I was away. Although it was a quick trip, it felt like two weeks," he said and leaned his head against hers.

"I agree," she replied and smiled.

Tony smiled too. "So, are you ready for our dinner date?" he then asked. "Well, you tell me," she replied and showed him her dress.

"Oh, I saw you when you walked out of the building," he said. "I was like, 'Dang… that's my babe, looking all good.' You had me in here smiling from ear-to-ear," Tony added.

"Really?" Jade questioned and began blushing. "I know you wanted me to wear something flattering for the evening so… I thought to wear this." She looked down at her dress.

"Which is a great choice, indeed. You look absolutely beautiful, and I can't wait to see you stand up again," he said, lightly brushing his thumb across her cheek.

Jade smiled. "So, where are we going?"

"You'll see," Tony politely replied. He then glanced out the window and realized they were just minutes from the restaurant. "Well, looks like you don't have to wait much longer to find out," Tony said and turned back to look at Jade.

She then glanced out the window to see what he was talking about. As the driver got closer to their destination, she began recognizing the area. While still in the heart of Manhattan, they slowly pulled up to the front lobby of a fairly tall building. Just seconds later, Tony realized the car stopped. He quickly checked his phone for messages, then he immediately put it away after not seeing anything too important.

"Ah, we're here," he said and softly tapped Jade's leg. "This is the place I selected for us to have dinner tonight, and it wasn't too long of a ride."

"Well, from what I see, you've definitely selected a nice location," Jade replied.

"Yeah, I wanted it to be somewhere special," he responded. They both gazed out the window while waiting for the driver to come and open their door.

"Ma'am," the driver said as he held the door open for them to get out. "Let me help you there, ma'am," he said to Jade and extended his hand.

"Why, thank you," she replied and made her way out of the limo. "Sir," the driver then said to Tony and held it open for him as well.

"Thanks," Tony said and pulled a fifty-dollar bill out of his pocket and handed it to the driver.

"Thank you, sir," the driver said and walked away.

"Jade, babe, right this way," Tony then said and took her by the arm. "I'm pretty sure this man can take us up," he added as they walked on the red carpet that led inside.

"Hello," said Jade and Tony. They both spoke to the host standing at the front entrance.

"We have reservations tonight for one of your rooftop tables," said Tony.

"Sure, you must be the special couple they've been waiting for," the host replied and led them to the elevator.

After fully entering what Jade learned was a very elegant hotel, she curiously began looking around the fancy, luxurious lobby. She noticed one of the desk attendants smiling when they walked past.

"Babe, this is a nice place, but you didn't have to do so much," Jade said and looked around at all the elegant décor.

"Oh, yes, I did," he softly replied and grabbed her hand. They stepped on the elevator, then the host pushed 12 on the panel, and it headed up to the rooftop level.

"Are you okay?" Tony asked and looked in Jade's direction. He then leaned and kissed her on the cheek before she answered.

"Yes, I'm fine, babe. You are just full of surprises," she replied and smiled.

"Look, you deserve the best, and that's what I want to deliver," Tony responded. The elevator doors finally opened, and Jade's mouth dropped after seeing what was before her eyes. She immediately looked at Tony in awe.

"What is all this?" Jade asked after admiring the beautiful ambiance and large windows. She then happened to notice that there was only one elegant-looking table in the room.

"This is for you, babe. You work so hard from running your own business, to taking care of the kids, and everything else in between. This is for you," he softly repeated, then he took her by the hand and led her further into the room.

"Oh, my God. The views of the Brooklyn Bridge and skyline are so beautiful from up here! You can see everything so good with all the big windows. I love it, babe. You really have great taste. I knew that when I first met you." Jade smiled. "Hey, remember how I teased you about your ring when we first met?"

"Oh, yeah, you really schooled me that night," Tony replied. "You actually gave me a hard way to go all night."

"Well…. look where we are now and still going strong," she responded as she leaned in to kiss his lips.

"Yes, I got you now, and you're not going anywhere. I plan to be with you for—." Suddenly, he stopped talking before finishing his sentence. "So, what do you think of the lighting?" he asked, quickly changing the subject.

"It's perfect. Everything is just perfect!"

"Good, I was hoping you'd love it." Tony then signaled for the waiter. "Tonight we're having champagne," he said and held out her chair for her to sit.

"Thank you, babe," she said and laid her wristlet on the table as she sat down, and he walked to his chair. "By the way, babe, you look some kind of good in that suit you're wearing."

"What? Oh, you're talking about this ole thing!" Tony looked down, pointing at his suit.

Jade shook her head and waved her hand. They both laughed as he took his seat. The waiter arrived at the table, holding a tray with two wine glasses, half-filled with champagne. "Wow, I guess he knew just what to bring out," Jade said and smiled.

"Yup, he sure did…" Tony replied with a grin. He then grabbed both glasses off the tray and handed Jade hers. "Let's toast to a special night," Tony said and raised his glass in the air.

"To a special night, it is," she replied and toasted her glass to his.

"So, how are the parents?" Tony asked out-of-the-blue.

"Oh, they're good. Mom has been busy with church activities, and dad is still his cool, laidback self," Jade answered.

"Well, good. Glad to hear they're doing fine," said Tony. He then took a sip of his champagne and looked over at Jade. "Hey, babe, would it be okay if I had your parents' number?" He randomly asked out-of-nowhere.

Jade slowly looked up after she took a sip of her champagne. "Uhm, my parents' number? May I ask what for?" Her tone was puzzling.

"Oh, absolutely," he answered. "I was thinking we give them a call."

"Oh, okay…" Jade replied even more puzzled by Tony's answer. He then pulled out his phone and laid it on the table.

"Now? You want to call them? Like, right now?" she asked, looking even more puzzled.

"Yup, I would like to say hello to them using video chat," Tony chuckled.

"You are something else."

Tony grabbed her hands and looked into her eyes. "I love you, and I want to love them too. Babe, I know it's not a formal introduction, but I don't want to put this off," he added.

"But, we're at dinner, babe. Can't we call them another day?" Jade asked.

"I would really like to do this now. Tonight," Tony sincerely replied. "Okay, if you insist," she said with a chuckle. Jade shook her head then read the number to Tony. He immediately dialed the number.

"I hope Mama knows how to answer a video chat call. I believe she and my brother used it before when they talked," she added. Tony hit 'Call,' and the phone started dialing. Jade looked at him and smiled. He, on the other hand, looked a little nervous.

"Hello," Mama said as her face appeared on the screen.

"Hi, Mama; it's Jade, and I have my friend, Tony, here with me."

"Oh, hi, baby. Is everything alright?" Mama asked.

"Yes, Mama. Everything is fine," Jade answered. "My friend, Tony, asked me to call you and Papa, so can you get him?"

"Sure, baby, one second." Mama called for Papa to come to the phone. Papa's face also appeared on the screen with Mama's. Tony then moved in closer, so they could see him and Jade both.

"Hello, Mr. and Mrs. Taylor. I'm Tony, the one your lovely daughter has told you about. Please know this is all my doing. Jade was very shocked when I asked her to call you," Tony explained. Jade smiled then leaned her head against his.

"Well, it is nice to at least meet the man that our daughter is dating," said Papa.

"I agree, sir," Tony replied.

"Where are you two at?" Mama asked after she noticed the elegant lighting in the background.

"Oh, we are at dinner, Mama," answered Jade.

"Dinner, and y'all called us?" Jade looked at Tony with a grin on her face, waiting to hear what his reply would be.

"Well, Mr. and Mrs. Taylor, I really wanted to meet you both, but there is one other reason why I asked Jade to call you." Tony waved his hand at the waiter. Jade then began to notice the ambience change in the dining room. The lights got a bit dimmer and soft sounds of a familiar love song started playing in the background.

"Tony, babe, what's going on here?" Jade whispered with curiosity.

The waiter walked over to the table and whispered in Tony's ear. "Is everything good, sir?" he asked.

Tony nodded. "Yes, thank you." The waiter walked away. Then Tony looked at Jade and smiled. He propped the phone on the table so Jade's parents could see them. "Mr. and Mrs. Taylor, can you see us clearly? I mean, can you see our body movements here at the table?" Tony asked excitedly—while deep down inside, he was really nervous.

"Yes, dear, we can see you both," answered Mama. "I can even hear the music in the background. Hey… I like that song," she then added and swayed her head to the music.

Jade smiled, shook her head, then looked back at Tony, still in question about what was going on. "Okay, good," he said. Then he took Jade's hands in his. "Mr. and Mrs. Taylor, I know this is your baby girl who you love dearly," Tony said softly, looking at them on the phone screen and back at Jade.

Jade smiled but remained silent. She stared in Tony eyes while she still wondered what was going on. "Well, Mr. and Mrs. Taylor, I love your J, too, and know deep within my heart that I sincerely want to spend the rest of my life with her."

"Tony, dear, that's nice you wanted to share that with us," Mama said.

"Yeah, thank you, son," said Papa. "I respect that in a man: reassuring her parents that you love their daughter," Papa added. Then both her parents smiled.

"Oh… absolutely, sir," Tony replied immediately. He then let go of Jade's hands, got up from his seat, and walked over near her. She shifted her position and turned toward him. The music that was playing got lower as Tony went down on one knee. Jade looked at him in awe.

"Babe, what are you doing?" she whispered. Tony reached in his suit pocket and slowly pulled out a small, black, velvet box. Jade immediately placed her hands over her mouth.

"Babe, you know I love you so much," he said softly. "I've never met a woman who I adore as much as you. You challenged me from the beginning, and you loved me too. Jade, my love, I know from this day forward that I couldn't dream of living my life without your presence," Tony added.

Jade got teary-eyed as she continued looking into his eyes. "I love you, too, babe," Jade replied softly.

Still on bended knee, Tony slowly opened the black box, took hold of Jade's left hand, and looked into her eyes. Jade's parents glanced at each other then quickly moved the phone closer to their faces to see where the conversation was leading. Meanwhile, the staff that Tony hired for the night all peeked out from the back to watch too.

"Babe, I know it may seem a little too soon for what I'm about to ask you, but a man knows when he's found that one," Tony then said. Jade smiled and wiped a tear from her eye. "Which is why I wanted your parents' number, so they can also be present when I ask.… Will you marry me?" He then held up a beautiful, three-carat, cushion-cut diamond ring.

There wasn't a sound in the room as everyone was silent and focused on Jade, waiting on her response. She looked at her parents then back at him with her teary eyes. There was a slight pause before she answered. *Thank You, Lord,* Jade thought.

"Yes, I will marry you!" Tony then took the ring and proudly placed it on her finger. They both stood, smiled with joy, and hugged each other. Everyone in the restaurant began cheering. Jade looked at the ring then immediately put her hand in front of the phone to show her parents. They both began to get teary-eyed, looked at Jade, and smiled.

"Congratulations, hon!" Mama said. Her dad nodded in agreement and smiled.

"Well, Mama and Papa, I guess we have a wedding to plan," Jade said. "We sure do!" Mama replied excitedly.

"Oh, my, I can't wait to tell the ladies!" Jade responded excitedly. "They are going to trip out when I show them this beautiful ring," she said, holding her hand out in front of her.

"So, you like your ring I take it?" asked Tony.

"Do I like it?" Jade replied, while still admiring its beauty.

Tony chuckled then signaled the waiter for dinner to be served. Right after that, he immediately took the phone in his hand. "Mr. and Mrs. Taylor, I'm so glad you were able to be a part of this very special moment. I really look forward to sharing my life with your daughter and the kids. They mean a great deal to me already," Tony expressed. "Also, I do know it was a little sudden, but I knew she was the one," said Tony.

"Well, you have our blessings, dear," Mama replied.

"Thank you," Tony replied.

"Well, Mama, we will let you two get back to your lives, and we will be in touch," Jade said and leaned her face in so they could see her.

"Okay, hon. You two enjoy the rest of your evening," said Mama as she waved goodbye. Papa also waved, but in the background, he struggled to see Jade's face before the call ended. She blew them a kiss and hung up the call.

Jade and Tony sat back down at the table to enjoy a romantic dinner and to finish off their champagne. They both admired the city view and slow-danced to the soft music playing. The two couldn't get enough of each other that night, and eventually, ended up losing track of time. After dancing and talking until around midnight, Tony happened to glance at his watch as he held Jade in his arms. "Babe… it's getting late. I better get you in the bed so you can get your beauty rest. I know you ladies have to get your beauty sleep."

"Yeah, I guess you're right, my future hubby," Jade said. She smiled and kissed his cheek.

"Hmmm… I like the sound of that," Tony replied. He then signaled for the waiter again while Jade grabbed her purse. Tony whispered in his ear. "Is her room ready?"

"Absolutely, sir. It's just as you requested," the waiter promptly replied.

"Great, thanks for your service this evening," said Tony, and he tipped the waiter. "Babe, you ready?" Tony asked.

Jade nodded and walked over near him. Tony took her by the hand then headed toward the elevators. "Since I knew we would probably be out late, I decided to get you a room here at the hotel," said Tony.

Jade looked at him with her tired eyes. "I love you…" she said and leaned her head on his shoulder. The elevator doors opened. Tony smiled as he lightly squeezed her hand; then they stepped on. He took Jade to her room, opened the door, then hugged and kissed her goodnight.

"Sweet dreams, babe," Tony said and took out his room key.

"Wait… where are you going?" Jade asked.

"Right here," he answered and stepped over to the room next to hers. Jade shook her head and smiled. *I love me some him,* she thought to herself. "I'll be right here, babe, if you need anything," Tony added.

"I should be fine," Jade said and looked around the beautifully-decorated room.

"Good!" said Tony, and they both closed their doors.

7

The winter passed as Jade and Tony prepared for their big day. "I'm getting married!" Jade shouted with excitement as she pranced around the boutique, admiring her ring. "Can y'all believe it?" she playfully questioned. "This is really happening to me—well, and the kids, too, of course. We will be a family soon. Jayden and Brittany will actually have a stepdad in the home."

"Yeah, girly, and now you'll have those wife responsibilities too! You know…. like, scrub your man's back, wash his dirty drawls, massage his stinky feet after a long day at work, and then do the—" said Sasha, but before she could finish, Jade stopped her.

"Alright!" she playfully yelled.

Zoe and Sasha both laughed, then Jade laughed too.

"For the record, my man's feet don't stink, and his drawls aren't dirty!" Jade exclaimed with one hand on her hip and waved the other at Sasha. "Also, I don't mind washing Tony's back, and well, the other responsibility… you already know!" she added.

They all laughed.

"Girly, we love you and are so happy for y'all," said Sasha as she walked over to Jade.

"Yes, we are and can't wait for your big day," Zoe added.

"So, girly, where y'all going for your honeymoon?" asked Sasha.

"We are going to Paris!" she replied excitedly. "We thought it would be the perfect honeymoon destination," Jade added.

"Wow, Paris. That's so romantic," said Zoe.

"Well, girly, just be sure to bring me a bottle of their French wine," said Sasha with a chuckle.

"Yeah, me too!" Zoe yelled. Then they all chuckled.

"Y'all are too funny, but I'll see what I can do. Anything for my girls." Jade was beaming. They all did a group hug before finishing the work around the boutique.

"Hey, let me see that gorgeous ring of yours again," requested Zoe. Jade held her hand out in front of Zoe and Sasha.

"Yeah, girly, he did good by picking out this one here," said Sasha as she looked closely at the ring.

"So, what do you think Blaine would say if he knew you were getting married?" asked Zoe.

Jade got quiet. "Wow, I don't know, and I can't really worry about that either," she replied. "Besides, he had his chance, and the reality is I now believe he just wasn't the one God had for me," Jade added.

Sasha and Zoe looked at one another and then at Jade. "Yup, she's right. No time to be worried about something that wasn't meant to be anyway," said Zoe in agreement.

"Oh, I'm not worried," replied Jade and walked over near the accessories. "Okay, ladies, let's get to work. We have to get this place looking nice before tomorrow's trunk show. By the way, I'm so glad tomorrow is Thursday because on Friday, Tony and I are finalizing everything for the wedding and picking up my parents from the airport."

"That's nice," said Zoe. "So, they'll get to spend a little time getting more acquainted before the wedding."

"Yes, which is a good thing," replied Jade and smiled.

"Girly, there is a lot to do before your big day," said Sasha. "So, we do need to get a move on things around here," she added.

"Yeah, I agree. Your wedding is this Sunday," said Zoe.

"Okay, but first, let me tell y'all how grateful I am to be working with one of the best wedding planners in New York City. Not only is she very professional, but patient too!" Jade excitedly said. "Plus, having you two, my BFFs, by my side means so much." Jade gave them both a hug. "Oh, wait, can't forget Mama and Papa and Tony's family's support. I wouldn't have been able to do this without you all. I'm even more grateful that Tony's side is paying for the majority of the wedding since that's where the most money is." Jade playfully tapped Sasha's arm.

"Yup. It sure is, but that's alright, girly!" said Sasha and nodded her head in agreement with Jade. They all laughed.

"Planning a wedding is a team effort, and I'm just so thankful that you are a part of my special day," said Jade. "Tony really wants everything to go smoothly and know that I'm happy. Plus, he wants to make sure our guests have a good time too.

"Oh, we don't think for a moment that man don't want to see you happy," said Zoe. "By the way, I was just thinking. I sure hope I get married one day," she added.

"I hope so, too, if that's what you want," replied Jade. Then she gave her a hug.

"Yeah, girly, someday," said Sasha. "I thank God for Mike and that he loves me the way I am!" Sasha jokingly said.

"Yes, Lord…" Jade said. They all laughed.

"Thanks, you guys. I'll just keep praying," Zoe added with a smile. "Okay, ladies, let's get busy. The day will be gone before we know it,"

Jade said as she checked the time. They all immediately got back to work.

Jade and Tony's big day had finally arrived.

"Who's helping Jade with her dress?" Mama asked.

"I think Sasha and Zoe are in the room helping her, Grandma," answered Jayden.

"Well, where's Tony?" she then asked.

"Oh, I saw him in the men's lounge area a few minutes ago," answered the wedding coordinator after she overheard her question.

Mama then yelled across the lawn. "Brittany!"

"I'm coming, Grandma!" she yelled back and ran over to her.

"Here, take these to your mother," Mama said and handed Brittany a pair of rhinestone, ankle-strap heels and a bag with accessories.

Papa then walked up and stood next to Jade's mama. "Everything is going to be fine. Calm down," he said and gave her a hug.

"It's just our J is finally getting married, and I want to help make sure everything goes as planned," Mama replied, wiping a tear from her eye.

"I know, and it will," said Papa.

Tony slowly walked over next to Jade's parents. "Hello, Mr. and Mrs. Taylor."

"Well, hello there, Tony. Don't you look handsome," said Jade's mama.

"Thank you, ma'am. It seems as if everyone on our guest list actually showed up," Tony said after he looked around at the crowd of people.

"Well, son, this is a beautiful venue you two selected—right here near the water," said Papa.

"Yes, and it's so nicely decorated," Jade's mama added.

"Yeah, this was Jade's idea, and I agreed it would be a nice place," replied Tony.

Then the wedding coordinator walked over and tapped Tony's arm. "Okay, quickly, places everyone!" she yelled and took one last look around the venue.

Shortly after the wedding coordinator made sure everyone was in place, she signaled for the pianist to start playing. Then she signaled for the bridesmaids and groomsmen to start walking. After everyone in the wedding party made their way down the aisle, she signaled again, but this time for Jade. The song then changed, and everyone stood as Jade and her papa walked down the aisle. She had on the most beautiful off-white, off-the-shoulder, crystal beaded, lace mermaid-style wedding dress.

"My babe looks so gorgeous," Tony whispered to his best man, Mike, after seeing her for the first time in her dress. All the guests were in awe at how beautiful Jade looked as she slowly made her way to the altar. Jade realized that she had to move to Manhattan, New York, to find true love, the love that she had always wanted.

THE END

About the Author

Chartese Mitchell grew up in the Maryland/Washington, DC, area. She is the owner of Brighter Star Press LLC publishing company, a mother of two young adults, and an author of two children's stories—working on a third! She developed a love for writing several years ago after writing her first poem. Yes, Chartese writes poetry as well. She has a little over 50 written poems of various types under her belt. The first book she wrote was a children's story, *In Due Time*, which came about after telling her children a bedtime story when they were younger. Chartese also has a love for fashion and style, which developed at a young age. She went to a local business institution, where she resided at the time, with a major in Office Automation. Then, she later attended and graduated from the School of Cosmetology and did hair on the side. Chartese even spent time as a shoe model for a fashion magazine in New York. When she's not writing and/or publishing her books, you could probably find her shopping in a mall or online.

"When I write, my goal is to entertain my readers. Whether it be through fictional characters or descriptive words, I like to indulge the imagination by taking my audience to other places of enjoyment, and at times, providing them with a little inspiration." - Chartese Mitchell